Big Bunny Bump-off

By

Kathi Daley

This book is a work of fiction. Names, characters, places, and incidents either are products of the author's imagination or are used fictitiously. Any resemblance to actual events or locales or persons, living or dead, is entirely coincidental.

This book is dedicated to my bunny-loving girls, Maleia and Maevelynn.

Special thanks to all my Facebook friends who share their opinions and encouragement, with a special thanks to Barbara H. for all the "likes" and comments.

And, as always, thank you to my sister Christy, for her encouragement and valuable feedback, Ricky for the webpage, Randy Ladenheim-Gil for the editing, and, last but not least, my super-husband Ken, for allowing me time to write by taking care of everything else.

Books by Kathi Daley

Paradise Lake Series:
Pumpkins in Paradise
Snowmen in Paradise
Bikinis in Paradise—coming May 2014

Zoe Donovan Mysteries:
Halloween Hijinks
The Trouble with Turkeys
Christmas Crazy
Cupid's Curse
Big Bunny Bump-off

Beach Blanket Barbie – coming April 1, 2014

Road to Christmas Romance:
Road to Christmas Past

Chapter 1

Sunday, March 23

"I told you this was a bad idea," Mom said as I fanned my dad's face with a magazine that I'd quickly folded to serve as a means of generating air flow.

"I guess you were right. It seemed like he was doing okay at first," I added as Mom gently lifted his head and slipped a pillow beneath it.

"I guess these things sort of sneak up on you." Mom ran her hand over dad's forehead, a look of concern on her face. "Do you think we should call the doctor?"

"I'm sure he'll be fine, but I'm afraid he's going to have one hell of a headache when he wakes up." I stopped fanning and sat back on my heels. "I have to say, I've never seen anyone sink to the ground in quite that manner. One minute he was sitting next to us on the sofa and the next he was slithering to the floor like a rag doll."

"He tried to warn us," Mom pointed out.

"I know." I sighed. "I just thought that if he tried it, he'd realize it really isn't that bad. I know how important this is to you."

"I appreciate the fact that you tried. I think he's opening his eyes."

"Zoe?" My dad looked at me. "What happened?"

"We were watching the video and you passed out," I answered.

"Oh God." Dad's hand flew to his mouth.

"It's okay," I encouraged him. "Just breathe. Deep breath in, slow breath out."

Dad did as instructed, but I have to admit that I've never seen anyone quite that shade of green.

"Okay, once again," I instructed. "Deep breath in, slow breath out."

"Should I get the bucket?" Mom asked.

"Yeah, that might be a good idea. Get a glass of water while you're at it," I added.

I looked back toward my dad, who was still taking long, deep breaths as my mom waddled toward the kitchen. He was looking better and his color had shifted from green to sort of a pale white. Maybe the bucket wouldn't be necessary after all. "Can you sit up?" I asked.

"Maybe." Dad tried to scoot up onto his forearms but winced and laid his head back down.

"Are you hurt?" I asked.

"I don't think so. I guess I'm still dizzy."

Mom hurried into the room and knelt down next to Dad's head. She helped him to sit and then held the glass, feeding him the water like one would a child.

I smiled at the domestic scene unfolding before me. Mom gently stroked Dad's cheek as he leaned back against the front of the sofa. I couldn't help but revel in the way the two people who had brought me into the world looked at each other with love in their eyes. It might have been a long and winding road to get here, but the one thing I'm sure of is that life is short and you need to cherish special moments when you have them rather than mourning the ones you might have missed along the way.

"What happened?" My boyfriend Zak came into the little boathouse I call home from the front drive, carrying the bags of groceries he'd offered to pick up.

"I borrowed the birthing video from Anyssa," I explained.

"Ah." Zak needed no further explanation.

"Maybe we should take him to the hospital to have him checked out," Zak suggested after he'd deposited the bags he'd carried in and joined us near the sofa.

"No, I'm fine." Dad smiled weakly. "I'm mostly just embarrassed."

"You were brave to try to watch the video," Mom consoled him. "A lot of men would have just made some joke about birthing being women's work and used it as an excuse to sit it out in the waiting room, rather than admitting to weakness of any kind."

Dad sat up the rest of the way and cupped Mom's cheek with his hand. "You, my dear, are kind. Too kind. I feel like I'm letting you down."

"Never," Mom said as she helped Dad onto the sofa he'd recently slithered off of. "Zoe is happy to fill in as coach."

"I am," I assured Dad. "In fact, I'm looking forward to it."

"I brought dinner," Zak announced as I noticed the takeout bags mixed in among the grocery bags for the first time.

"I'm starving." I got up from my position on the floor, walked over to the tile counter that separated my small kitchen from the living area, and dug into the white paper bags.

"Me too." Mom stood up from where she was still sitting on the floor. "Hank?" she asked my dad.

"I'm feeling better. I think I can eat. What did you bring?"

"Chinese," Zak informed us.

Dad started to turn green again.

"Maybe some white rice to start," I suggested.

"Yeah, that might be a good idea," Dad agreed.

Mom helped Dad to his feet, not an easy feat for a petite woman who was over eight months pregnant. Mom and I have similar features. While I have curly brown hair and hers is straight blond, we both have blue eyes, wide smiles, and tiny frames that tip the height chart at just about five feet. While we normally weigh less than a hundred pounds fully clothed, Mom *has* put on a few pregnancy pounds. Very few. I hope that, if and when I become a mother, I look as beautiful as she does. From the back, you'd never even know Mom was with child; it's only the basketball under her bright yellow peasant blouse that informs people that she's going to be a mother again in less than a month.

"What did you do with the dogs?" I asked when I realized that my dog Charlie and Zak's dog Lambda had gone with Zak when he headed into town but hadn't followed him when he came inside.

"They're on the deck with Tucker and Kiva," Zak said, referring to Dad's two dogs. "I figured four dogs in your little house were going to be tight, and it's a nice day."

I looked out of the window. It *was* a nice day. The sun was just beginning to set over the glassy lake, which was filled to the brim with melting snow. We'd had a heavy winter that I'd been beginning to think would never end, but today had been sunny and warm, and I'd felt my heart fill with joy brought on by the arrival of spring.

I looked at my mom and dad. It seemed fitting that my baby sister would be born in the spring, the season of new birth. After my dad got over the shock of my mom's pregnancy, the two of them had decided to take things slow as they worked out the parameters of their new relationship. When I had been born, my mom had handed me off to my dad and then pretty much exited from my life. This time around, Mom wanted to be a real mother, while still allowing Dad to be a full-time father. The pair had a lot of murky water under their bridge, and I knew it would take a while for them to work things out. Still, my deepest hope is that my baby sister will grow up in the same house as *both* of her parents.

"Have you thought any more about the house I showed you?" Zak asked as he dished the food he'd brought into serving bowls.

Zak had found a beachfront home that's larger than my tiny one-bedroom boathouse but much smaller than his almost twenty-thousand-foot lakefront mansion. We'd looked at it a few days ago and realized it would be perfect for my parents. Mom and Dad want to parent together, though both had stopped short of admitting they were ready to become a couple. (Like I said, there are deep, deep rivers of unresolved feelings for them to deal with.) The property Zak had found had two structures. The main house has three bedrooms, two baths, and a large kitchen and open living area. Just across the pool and patio area is a mother-in-law unit, with one bedroom and one bath, plus a smaller yet still roomy living area. The space seemed perfect for Dad to live in until they realized they really were in love and should move in together.

"I like it, but I'm not sure I can afford it," Dad stated as he helped himself to a generous helping of sweet and sour pork to go with the rice I'd suggested.

"I told you not to worry about the money," Mom answered. (Did I mention that my mom is filthy rich?)

"I've always paid my own way and will continue to do so," Dad insisted.

"If you sell the house you're living in now, you should be able to pay for your share," I pointed out as I dug into my shrimp chow mein. "Mom will actually have over two-thirds of the living space, so . . ." I left the conclusion unstated but hoped Dad would jump on the logic of footing only a third of the bill.

"It's a beautiful spot," Mom said persuasively. "And it's just down the beach from Zoe. Harper and I can walk down the beach any time she wants to see her big sister."

"Well, I guess it could work for our situation," Dad admitted. "And it is on a large lot, with a fenced-in area for the dogs and a big garage for all my tools. I don't like the idea of you living alone, and I suppose you can't live with Zak forever."

Mom had been living with Zak since she came back to town, which had caused all kinds of jealousy on my part until I found out that the woman he had living with him was actually my mother. When I first discovered the truth, I passed out dead in the snow. Perhaps a weak constitution and a tendency toward fainting runs in the family.

"The guy who owns the place is a friend of mine." Zak topped off the wine for the three of us not with child, while I refilled Mom's water glass. "He's really motivated to sell quickly. I guess he took some bad investment advice and lost a bucketful of his cash reserves, so he's eager to sell the property to pay off some of his mounting debt. If you're interested, I can have a chat with him to see if we can work out something on the price."

I knew that translated into Zak slipping the guy some money under the table so my dad could afford his share of the house and suspected Dad knew that as well, but he had the common sense not to say as much. You see, as rich as Mom is—and she's *very* rich—Zak is richer. He built a software company in the garage when he was a teenager that he then sold for tens of millions of dollars when he was twenty-one. He's continued to dabble in the software industry, and to tell you the truth, I have no idea how much he's actually worth.

"Negotiating the price down would help," Dad admitted. "Still, my house is paid for, and it's in a nice location close to town. I should be able to get a good price for it."

"Carson and I go way back and he's a reasonable guy. I'll talk to him," Zak offered again. "I'm sure he'll welcome the chance to avoid the hassle of putting his house on the open market. I think the house will be perfect for your situation, and it's close to Donovan's,"—he referred to the general store Dad and my grandfather, Pappy, own—"so even when you're at work, you won't be far away. It's basically turnkey, so I may even be able to work it out so you can move in right away."

"I still need to sell my house," Dad reminded Zak. "That could take a while."

"I'm pretty sure Carson will agree to finance the venture as long as the down payment is enough to take care of his immediate needs," Zak said. "Madison can foot the down payment and when you sell your house, you can contribute to the total. It really could be a win-win. You can get settled before the baby is born, and Carson can make a little extra on the interest."

"Does that work for you?" Dad looked at Mom.

"Absolutely."

"Okay." Dad smiled. "Let's see what we can work out."

"I'm so excited," I said, beaming. "This is going to be awesome." Despite my genuine enthusiasm about the imminent arrival of my baby sister, I'm pretty nervous. You see, babies—at least human ones—terrify me. It may be due to the fact that I'm an only child and have never spent much time around the squirmy little noise boxes. Mom seems nervous as well, so I've been pretending that I'm a baby-raising pro whenever she's around.

"Does anyone need anything else?" Zak asked as we scarfed down the food he'd arranged on my little dining table.

"I think we're good," I answered as I reached for seconds.

"So how was play rehearsal?" he asked, changing the subject to something less emotionally charged than babies and finances.

The community theater, which is operated by fellow events committee member Gilda Reynolds, is putting on an Easter play as part of our annual Spring Fling event. My best friend, Ellie Davis, who runs an afterschool dance program and is co-directing the play, asked me to help out. Ellie has done me so many favors over the past few months that I can't even keep up with how many I owe her back, so I readily agreed to pitch in. Which, I realized in hindsight, might have been a mistake. The use of the word *chaos* to describe the entire undertaking is putting it mildly. Things started off okay until bank president Porter Blakely insisted on playing the part of Jack Frost. There are several problems with this scenario, the least of which is that Jack Frost is considered to be a thin, fairylike figure, while Blakely, decisively, is not (think of a hippo in a tutu).

The second problem we faced is that the theater group is putting on an Easter play and not a Christmas one, so the character of Jack Frost wasn't in the original script. But Blakely has money and power and, apparently, some unresolved childhood Jack Frost issues, so Gilda cleverly rewrote the script to accommodate the man who holds the mortgages to most of the businesses in town, including Gilda's touristy-type shop, Bears and Beavers.

Dad said, "Gilda did a fabulous job of coming up with a script to accommodate Blakely's tantrum."

"What did she do?" Mom asked.

"Basically," I answered, "it's a story about how Jack Frost mourns the end of winter and the coming of spring each year, so he comes up with a way to stop spring from coming, creating a sort of endless winter. The play explores a monotonous world, resulting in dramatic changes to everything we know."

"Sounds awful." Mom laughed.

"Tell me about it." I was already so, so done with snow and cold temperatures. If I didn't know that summer was just around the corner, I don't know what I'd do. "Anyway, the story is about the Easter Bunny and his attempt to find a way to save spring.

It's sort of corny, but it *does* have an Easter theme, and it *does* make Blakely happy, and it even provides for an identifiable theme people can relate to."

"Who'd they finally get to play the Easter Bunny?" Dad asked. Frank Valdez, the owner of Outback Hunting and Fishing and the organizer for the outdoor summer camp for underprivileged kids, normally took the part of the Easter Bunny in the annual play and owned his own costume, but when Blakely came on board, he bowed out. I'm not privy to all the details, but the word around town is that Frank and Blakely entered into some sort of business arrangement that ended in a feud reminiscent of the Hatfields and McCoys.

"You'll never guess in a million years," I challenged.

"Pappy," Dad said.

"How'd you know?" I wondered. "Gilda just announced it today."

"I didn't know," Dad admitted. "I just thought of the least likely person to do it and Pappy came to mind. How did Gilda talk him into it?"

"She didn't. Hazel did."

Hazel Hampton, a woman in her early sixties, is the town librarian, a member of the events committee, and the chairperson of the book club Pappy and I belong to. If you ask me, Pappy might be developing feelings toward the friendly woman. He hasn't dated at all since Grandma died, but during the past few months, I've noticed a very gradual change in his reclusive ways. He even played Santa at Christmas, when the "real" Santa was in a car accident and the backup one was murdered.

"You don't say?" Dad smiled. "Well, good for her. Is Pappy going to wear the entire outfit?"

"Head and all," I confirmed.

"This I have to see." Dad chuckled. "And what part are you playing?"

"I'm firmly planted behind the scenes, monitoring sets, costumes, and pretty much anything I could volunteer for that wouldn't require me to set foot on the stage during the performance."

"That's too bad." Zak laughed. "I'm sure you would have made an adorable Easter egg."

"In your dreams." I threw an eggroll at him.

"It's funny you should say that," Dad commented. "Zoe actually *was* an Easter egg in the Easter play when she was five. And you're right, she was adorable."

"I'd forgotten all about that," I said with a laugh. "Now that I think about it, I do remember the tantrum I threw when I was assigned the role of a pink egg and wanted to be blue."

"Yeah, you never did like pink as a child."

"I feel so bad that I missed that." Mom sat back in her chair, looking down at her hands as a tear rolled down her cheek. "I missed so many precious moments I can never get back. I don't know what I was thinking."

"Don't worry, I'm sure Harper will be asked to be an egg when she's four or five. It's a bit of a town tradition," I said, offering encouragement. Mom had been *very* emotional lately, something I'd pretty much decided to chalk up to pregnancy hormones.

"Do you have pictures of your performance?" Mom asked.

I looked at Dad. "Do we?"

"Of course. We have pictures of everything." He turned to look at Mom. "I'll dig them out for you." I noticed that Dad was holding Mom's hand under the table, giving it an occasional squeeze of support. "It'll be fun to go through them all again. Maybe we can organize them into albums."

"I'd like that." Mom smiled.

"Before I forget to tell you," Zak turned to me, "I hired a contractor to come out and take a look at your siding."

"What's wrong with my siding?" I asked.

"The wood on the back of the boathouse needs to be refinished before it starts to rot. The challenge is to match the natural wood so as not to affect the integrity of the historic structure while using a sturdy enough product to protect it from the wind and moisture the wall that faces the lake endures every winter."

While I've never been the sort who longs to be taken care of, I was sort of enjoying the fact that I had Zak to worry about stuff like wood siding. I love the little boathouse I converted into living space several years ago, but I have to be honest and admit that I have no clue whatsoever when it comes to maintenance of the historic building. The converted space is small and generally easy to take care of, with a single room on the bottom floor featuring a living area arranged around huge picture windows overlooking the lake, a mere twenty feet from my back deck. A floor-to-ceiling river-rock fireplace provides warmth and a cozy feel on a cold winter's day, and thick walls of natural wood keep the little cabin insulated against cool alpine mornings. The kitchen is divided from the living area by a tile counter where I've placed bar stools for additional seating. There's a small bathroom off the kitchen, as well as a sleeping area located in the loft above the kitchen.

"I think I really need to be going," Mom said, massaging her lower back.

"I can drop you at Zak's," my dad offered.

"That's okay. I have some work to do and should probably get going myself," Zak responded.

"Are you sure?" I asked. "It's a beautiful night. We could build a fire in the pit out back and have a glass of wine."

Zak hesitated. "I guess it is a nice night."

Dad laughed. "I'll take Madison home. You kids have a nice evening."

Zak built a fire in the pit on the beach while I poured the wine. The last of the snow had finally melted from the basin, although there was still quite a bit of it on the mountains. Still, the beach was clear, and with the fire, the chilly spring evening was really quite pleasant. I grabbed a blanket to spread out under the stars, which shone brightly in the clear sky.

"It's so beautiful out here at night." I sighed contently.

"It really is. We should take a trip this summer. I know an island in the Pacific where the stars look close enough to reach out and touch. It's a lovely spot, with excellent scuba diving and wide white-sand beaches."

"It sounds wonderful, but I'm not sure how long it's going to be before I can go anywhere," I reminded Zak. "With Jeremy having a new baby, I won't be able to count on him to fill in like I have in the past."

"I've been thinking that we need to hire a few more people. Someone to cover, so that you and Jeremy can take time off, as well as someone to help out with the cleaning and heavier chores."

"That would be nice," I admitted. "I'd love to have someone on the premises 24/7, if we can work it into the budget. We never had a night shift when the county owned the facility, but now that we're talking on so much wildlife, many of which need monitoring and medical care, it would be helpful to have someone there all the time."

Zak began running his fingers through my hair, making it difficult for me to concentrate on the subject at hand. Not only is Zak a large man, at well over six feet four inches in height, but he has big hands that seem to know just how to touch me to cause my entire body to tingle from the top of my head to the bottom of my toes (and everywhere in between).

"You know, if we built a shed out back and moved the items that are now stored in the room in the back into it, we could convert that room into a bedroom," Zak suggested. "Maybe we can find a couple of people willing to do a graveyard shift."

"Hmm." I closed my eyes and relaxed as Zak's gentle caress sent tingles to all the best places.

"The more I consider the idea, the more I like it. Why don't you go ahead and advertise for three positions: a full-time day position, a graveyard position, and someone who can be flexible and maybe work two nights and three days. I'd like to get people hired and trained before Jeremy's baby is born so you don't end up living down there," Zak instructed.

"'Kay," I purred.

"Are you still listening to me?" Zak leaned down and kissed me.

I wrapped my arms around his neck and pulled him onto the blanket next to me. "Tell me later," I whispered as his lips found mine and all thoughts of employees and wild animals were replaced by something much more delightful.

Chapter 2

Friday, April 4

"This really couldn't get any worse," I groaned as Blakely strutted around the stage with his portly body poured into blue tights and a short white costume styled after the original fairylike Jack Frost. He had on moccasin-type shoes and a pointy hat that draped like a jester's.

"I thought you were in charge of costumes," Levi, the third member of the Zoe, Levi, and Ellie triad, pointed out. The two of us were seated in the community center, watching a rehearsal of the play Gilda had managed to put together after Blakely had forced us to make changes.

"I am, but Blakely insisted on providing his own. The man actually believes he looks good. He claims to have done quite a bit of research into the classic images of his favorite fantasy character and had a costume custom made to portray what he remembers from his childhood. The problem is that the original Jack Frost was small, thin, and fairylike. Blakely is tall and rotund. I'm flabbergasted they even make tights in his size. Gilda, Hazel, Ellie, and I have all tried to talk to him about designing a costume with pants and a jacket, similar to what Jack Frost wore in the *Santa Clause* movie, but he's having none of it."

"Maybe if someone of the male persuasion had a chat with him . . ." Levi suggested.

"Actually, Rob made a comment about tights being less than flattering for men, but Blakely insisted that the 'real' Jack Frost wore tights, so he would too."

"This whole thing is bizarre," Levi admitted. "Blakely is a bank president, for God's sake. He understands the importance of having a professional image. I can't believe he'd even think of prancing around in tights."

"If you ask me, Blakely has some sort of Jack Frost obsession left over from his childhood. He keeps making comments about now the 'real' Jack Frost would dress or what the 'real' Jack Frost would say. Rob and I talked about it, and we both agree Blakely actually seems to think there is a *real* Jack Frost. It's absurd."

"It sounds like he's lost his mind. Do you think he's dangerous?" Levi wondered.

"Rob doesn't think so. He minored in psychology in college, so he knows a bit about this stuff, and he seems like a pretty perceptive guy. He thinks Blakely's obsession is harmless, but to tell you the truth, I'm not so certain. The whole thing gives me the creeps, and with more than eighty percent of the cast being children, I think we should keep an eye on him."

"I'm surprised Ellie didn't enlist Rob to be in the play," Levi commented as Blakely leapt through the air like some sort of hippo ballerina. "He's been following her around like a puppy of late."

"Rob is more of a loving golden retriever than a puppy," I broke it to Levi, as Pappy, who wasn't dressed in costume since this wasn't even a dress rehearsal, began to enlist the support of the children in his battle to defeat Jack and save spring.

"Either way you slice it, he's a dog."

"Jealous much?"

"I'm not jealous. I'm just not sure that a man who is a good five years older than Ellie, with a young daughter to care for, is right for her. She needs someone more like . . ."

"More like you?"

"Exactly."

"Ellie loves Hannah, and she really likes Rob. They have a lot of fun together and he's very good to her. You really need to learn to like the guy if you want to maintain a relationship with Ellie in the long run."

Levi turned to look at me. "You think he's a long-run kind of guy?"

"Yeah. I do." I placed my hand over his arm. "It's much too early to tell where the relationship will lead, but Rob seems to be a plant-roots, raise-a-family, forever kind of guy, and I think Ellie likes that about him."

Levi frowned. I felt bad for him, but when he could have had Ellie, he'd been too busy panting after every blonde with long legs and a big chest. Rob wasn't as fun as Levi, but he was sweet and loyal, and he seemed to really care about Ellie, which made him okay in my book.

"So where is *your* lapdog today?" Levi asked in a snarky tone.

"Zak is not my lapdog," I snapped back.

"Sorry, I guess that was rude. I like Zak. You know I do, it's just that . . ." Levi looked toward the stage, where Ellie was explaining to some of the kids where they were supposed to stand.

"Yeah, I get it," I sympathized. "Zak is out of town on business, but he should be home this evening. He promised to be back in time to help my dad and mom move into their new place this weekend."

"Wow. That was fast. How'd they swing it to move in so quickly?"

"Zak knows the guy, and he worked out a deal. I'm pretty sure it consisted of an exchange of money, but we aren't advertising that to Dad, who is feeling sensitive about the financial aspect of the deal."

"Makes sense. Zak is loaded, your mom is loaded, and your dad has busted his butt his whole life, but no matter how hard he works, he'll never be able to compete."

"I don't think it's a competition."

"Really? I think for your dad it certainly is. He isn't the type of guy who wants to be kept."

Levi had a point. I'd pretty much bought, wrapped, and delivered the idea that Mom and Dad would be a *real* couple once they worked things out, but Mom was born into money and would always be rich, and Dad . . . well, short of winning the lottery, he most likely never would.

"I heard there's a storm coming in on Sunday. You might want to complete the move on Saturday, before it hits. I can help if you want."

"It's going to rain?" I asked.

"Actually, they're calling for snow. Up to a foot," Levi informed me.

"You can't be serious."

"Afraid I am."

"It's April."

Levi looked toward the stage. "Guess you should have a chat with Jack."

"Yeah, I guess I should. A foot of snow is really going to put a damper on Ellie's grand opening next week."

"Did she get everything worked out with Blakely?" Levi asked.

"Not really, but she decided to go along with the ridiculous contract and continue forward while their attorneys work out the details."

For those of you who aren't aware, Ellie and her mom, Rosie, recently secured a loan from the Ashton Falls Community Bank, of which Blakely is the president, to open a second location of the extremely popular Rosie's Café. Ellie has worked for her mother at the main restaurant since she was old enough to do so, and Rosie'd decided it was time for her daughter to have her own place. The location on the pier, near one of the most popular beaches in the area, is priceless. The new building is small, but Ellie had plans to make the most of the space and had been remodeling for the past few months. Shortly after she announced a grand-opening date, she'd learned that there was fine print in the contract she'd signed with the bank that gave Blakely control over management decisions regarding the enterprise. To say that both Ellie and Rosie are less than thrilled about this turn of events is putting it mildly. Zak helped them hire an attorney, but the truth of the matter is, they'd signed what they'd signed.

"I can't believe Blakely wants input on the menu," Levi complained. "Seems picky and petty to me."

"He claims that because the loan is unsecured, he's taking a big risk on the venture. He feels it's within his rights to ensure that decisions regarding the establishment that may affect the bottom line are made in the best interest of maintaining a certain profit margin. I know it's crazy, but the man is smart, and he included wording in the fine print that legally backs up his claim. Looking back, I guess Ellie should have run the loan contract past an attorney before she signed it, but the process took so long, she was just happy to get it finalized."

"I heard Blakely has been requiring Ellie to bring him samples of every item she intends to include on the menu."

"You heard right. If the guy continues to be such a huge tool, I can see how her next submission may be arsenic soup."

"If she wants to off Blakely, she might have to wait in line," Levi commented. "I ran into Walter Gates the other day, and he made a similar comment about wanting the guy gone. I guess things got a little tight over the winter, so he applied for a small line of credit to get him through until the tourism season. He told me that he's had to make similar requests a few times in the past, when winters have been particularly long or hard and they haven't had a lot of business at the resort, but this year Blakely handed him a loan agreement with all sorts of strange requirements that sound a lot like what he's pulling on Ellie."

"Wouldn't you think he'd have enough to do without wanting to have his hands in everyone's business?"

"It would seem so, but apparently Blakely is more of a control freak than anyone was giving him credit for."

"What did Walter do?" I wondered.

"He took his business elsewhere. I think Blakely's strange agreements are going to hurt him now that the word is out about what he's doing. Walter used to run a lot of money through his bank, but he's pulled all his deposit accounts as well as his loans."

Walter Gates owned the largest resort on the lake. In the summer months, the campground and small cabins were booked to capacity, but during the colder winter months the resort catered to just a few guests willing to stay in the rustic lodge. Not only did Walter own the largest resort on the lake but the largest marina as well. Blakely was an idiot to mess with a man who had the financial means and reputation Walter did.

"Do you think there's something more going on with Blakely than meets the eye?" I asked.

"What do you mean?"

"I don't know. The man has always been a little odd, but it's only been over the past six months or so that he seems to have completely gone off the deep end. First the strange loans and now the Jack Frost thing. Maybe he's suffered a mental breakdown of some type."

"Terrific. That's just what everyone wants to hear about the person who's holding their money. Luckily, I don't have any discretionary income, so the whole thing doesn't affect me, but if I did have money, I'd be thinking about taking Walter's lead and looking for another financial institution."

"Yeah, especially in this day and age, when it's so easy to bank online. It wasn't that long ago that proximity to your residence was an important feature in a bank, but not so much anymore. Maybe I should start looking for a new home for my meager savings as well."

"I'm sure Zak has his millions spread around. Maybe you can ask him for some suggestions."

"That's a good idea, although I try to avoid talking finances with Zak."

"Why is that?"

I leaned back into my chair as the choir came out onto the stage for the last number. "I don't know. He has so much of it. I guess the thought of all that money sort of freaks me out, so I try to focus on the things I love about Zak and not the things I would really rather do without."

"You'd rather Zak didn't have all that beautiful money?"

"Most of the time," I admitted.

"If he wasn't rich, he couldn't have bought the Zoo for you," Levi reminded me.

"True."

"And he wouldn't have that spectacular home with the pool and spa you love so much."

"Maybe. But he wouldn't be gone all the time, and he might not have *every* woman in the country panting after him."

"Perhaps. But then again, maybe he'd be gone all the time anyway, trying to make a meager living, and maybe his height and rugged good looks alone would still get the female attention you would just as soon didn't exist."

"Rugged good looks?" I laughed. "Perhaps it's not just the women in town who are crushing on him."

Levi grinned. "It's not so much a crush as the fact that we babe magnets tend to recognize one another."

I punched Levi playfully in the arm. "You're such a snob."

"Ouch, that hurt. You've got quite an arm for such a tiny thing." Levi rubbed his arm. "Want to get a drink when you're done here? Your treat for abusing me."

I laughed at Levi's attempt to portray the injured party. "Sure, that would be nice."

"I guess we should ask Ellie as well."

"Maybe we should." I grinned.

"What's with the smile?"

"I can't smile?" I tried to sound innocent, even though we both knew I was teasing him for his obvious interest in spending some time with Ellie.

Levi frowned. "I'm not sure I like this weirdness that's becoming more obvious between the three of us lately. I miss the old us. The us that used to tease one another and fake boxing matches all the time."

"We were kids when we used to punch each other on a regular basis, but I know what you mean. It seems like there's been a lot of change in the past few months. It'll be nice for the three of us to hang out. I've been spending all my time with Zak, and Ellie has been spending all her time with Rob, and you? Who exactly have you been spending all your time with?"

Levi shrugged. "No one in particular."

"Really? Levi Denton, the Casanova of Ashton Falls, has been living the single life?"

"Well, I haven't been a monk. I've dated, just not the same person more than once or twice."

"I see. Maybe being single for a while will be good for you. Have you heard from Barbie?"

"No. After we broke up and she moved away, she seems to have cut all ties with Ashton Falls. I even asked a few of her girlfriends if they'd heard from her, and they said they hadn't."

"I guess that's good."

"Maybe, but she left on such a strange note, I keep waiting for the other shoe to drop."

The rehearsal was over and the actors were beginning to disperse. I waved to Ellie, who acknowledged my gesture with one of her own, putting up a finger to let me know she'd be just a moment.

"What do you mean?" I asked Levi.

"I don't know exactly. It's probably just my imagination, but I have this feeling I haven't seen the last of her, and that when she does show up again, it's going to be like the sequel to a really bad horror flick: twice as bad as the first."

"I wouldn't worry about it. I doubt she'll be back, and if she is, I'm sure she will have moved on."

"Yeah, I guess. I've been thinking about asking out Carly Wilder again. We had a great time together at our birthday party, but at the end of the evening, when I mentioned getting together again, she seemed sort of evasive. I don't suppose you know her story?"

Levi had first hooked up with Carly Wilder at the Sweetheart Dance on Valentine's Day, when they'd both shown up alone. They hadn't seen each other again until the joint birthday party Zak had thrown for Levi and me a few weeks ago. My birthday is on March 10 and Levi's is on March 8, so we often celebrate together. Ellie had invited Carly, who'd seemed thrilled at the chance to renew her friendship with Levi, although the two hadn't hooked up since. Although Carly is two years younger than Levi and me, she's mature and settled, whereas Levi tends to focus on having fun and mixing things up. In my opinion, the two aren't really suited, and I think Carly realizes that.

"I don't know Carly really well," I answered. "I do know that she recently graduated with a nursing degree and is looking for a job. I imagine she'll leave the area once she finds what she's looking for."

"I'm just looking for a date, not a wife," Levi reminded me.

"Maybe you should ask Ellie about her. They took the same dance classes for years, so Ellie knows her better than I do. And I suppose if all you're looking for is a date, it couldn't hurt to ask. All she can do is say no."

Chapter 3

Monday, April 7

It had been a long and labor-intensive weekend, but Mom and Dad were moved into their new home and Zak and I finally had some privacy. Not that I hadn't relished the fact that having Mom living with Zak had given me the opportunity to really get to know her, but it had also thrown off the equilibrium we'd just begun to establish before she arrived. I love Zak, and I assume that someday we'll discuss the idea of a permanent living arrangement, but for now the ability for each of us to have our own space and share as we choose seems to be the best option.

"Are we expecting a delivery?" I asked my assistant, Jeremy Fisher, after I arrived at Zoe's Zoo, the wild and domestic animal control, rescue, and rehabilitation center we run.

"Bunnies," Jeremy answered as he cleaned one of the larger pens we normally used for wildlife. "Lots of them."

"Lots as in how many?" I was afraid to ask.

"The woman I talked to made it sound like there were hundreds. The county is shutting down a breeder in the valley for refusing to adhere to regulations regarding cleanliness and odor control. The Bryton Lake animal control facility is booked to the gills as usual, so they've asked us to dispose of the livestock."

"Hundreds?" I paled. "How are we going to find homes for hundreds of rabbits?"

"Well, they were raised as livestock," Jeremy pointed out.

"You think we should butcher them? Over my dead body."

"Don't have a coronary. I was just kidding, and I'm not sure there are actually hundreds, though there are quite a few. We should think about a special adoption clinic. At least it's Easter and people are looking for bunnies."

"A special adoption drive would be a good idea. Once we take possession of our new guests, have Scott look at them to make sure they're healthy, and then work up an ad we can run in all of the newspapers and social media sites in the area. Maybe we can find no-kill facilities in other areas that might be willing to take a few as well."

"Okay, I'm on it. By the way, a reporter from Channel 2 called and wants to do a feature story on the Anderson fire cubs. I told her you'd call her back."

"They've put on a lot of weight and look significantly better than when we first got them six weeks ago. I suppose it could be good publicity for the facility. Perhaps we can work in a mention of the bunnies."

"Her number is on the pad on your desk. Oh, and Ellie called. She said your cell was off. She wants you to call her as soon as possible. She said it's important."

I pulled my phone out of my pocket and looked at it. It *was* off. I'd really been working at being better about remembering to turn it on after I charged it, but apparently some bad habits die hard. I powered it up and saw that I had eight messages, four of which were from Ellie. I punched in her cell number and waited for her to answer.

"Thank God you called," Ellie answered after the first ring. "I need a favor. A big one."

"Sure, anything you need."

"I have to go to the county offices in Bryton Lake this afternoon to deal with a small kink in the outdoor permits for Ellie's Beach Hut, and I promised Blakely I'd drop by the final menus for him to look at after the bank closed for the day. The menus are at the printers and won't be done until after three, so I can't drop them by early. It would be a huge help if you could pick them up from the printer and then drop them off at the bank on your way home from the Zoo. Blakely said he'd be there late and would be listening for you to buzz him from the delivery entrance. I've done it before. There's an intercom on the outside wall just to the right of the door. All you have to do is push the button and speak. Blakely will come and let you in."

"Absolutely, no problem."

"Thanks. With all the snow we got yesterday, I really want to get down to the county early enough to do what I need to do and be back before dark."

"Yeah, that's a good idea. I heard we're expecting more snow this afternoon to go with the almost two feet we got yesterday. Maybe while I'm at the bank I can have a chat with Ol' Jack about laying off the snow machine," I teased.

"Seriously," Ellie agreed. "My plan for the opening was to feature both the indoor and the outdoor seating areas. Now I'm seriously thinking about postponing the event."

"I wouldn't worry too much. Spring snow usually doesn't stick around too long. It could very well be sixty degrees by the time you open on Friday."

"Here's hoping. And thanks again. Tell Blakely that if he has any questions, he can call me tomorrow."

"Will do."

"Everything okay?" Jeremy asked after I hung up.

"Yeah. Ellie just needs me to run an errand for her later this afternoon."

"Do you have time to go over the applications we received this week?"

"Certainly. Anyone look promising?"

"A few." Jeremy had organized the files so that the best candidates were on the top. He opened the first file so we could both view it together. "This application is from a woman who moved into my apartment building several months ago. Her name is Tiffany Middleton and she's twenty-three years old. She worked at an animal control center in Tampa, Florida, for two years and has a certificate in dog training as well.

"Why'd she move to Ashton Falls?" I wondered.

"She came here last winter to go skiing with some friends and fell in love with the place. She cashed in her savings, quit her job, and moved to the area just after the first of the year. She's currently working as a waitress but would really like to get back into working with animals. She asked me about getting a job here when she first arrived, but we hadn't reopened yet, so I told her that we didn't have anything for her. She seems enthusiastic and eager to work. We've had several discussions about how to handle problem animals, and I think she'll fit in with our overall philosophy really well."

"Sounds good. Let's set up an interview."

"Actually, I was hoping you could talk to her today. If you have time, that is. I really think she'll be great, and with Morgan on the way, I'd like to get someone trained so I don't leave you hanging while I'm off on my daddy leave."

"Okay. Call her up and ask her to come in. Who else do we have?"

"Lilly Evan's grandson Bobby is interested in the cleaning job. He can work weekends and every day after school, if we need him. He just got his driver's license and seems motivated to earn some money to buy a car."

"I know Bobby. He's a good kid. If you think he'll work out, go ahead and have him come in and do the paperwork. You can get started training him right away."

"Perfect." Jeremy smiled. "And last but not least, I only got one application from someone interested in the graveyard shift. To be honest, I'm not certain if this will be a good option or not. Two brothers applied and want to share the job, taking turns sleeping over. It seems they live together and figure that each will have their small cabin to themselves on the night the other is at the Zoo."

"Let me guess—Tank and Gunner Rivers?"

"How did you know?"

"Ashton Falls is a small town. It wasn't hard to whittle down the candidates and figure out which set of brothers sharing a cabin might be interested in the job."

"They're a little rough around the edges," Jeremy warned.

Jeremy wasn't wrong about the men being rough around the edges. Tank and Gunner were middle-aged twin brothers who worked together running fishing charters in the summer and doing snow removal in the winter. They lived in the same tiny cabin where they were raised. Their parents had died in an automobile accident when they were eighteen, and they'd stayed on in the cabin when they'd graduated high school. Neither had ever married, so both were still in residence. I'd need to look at the application to be certain, but I'd be willing to bet that the men were forty-five or forty-six.

Both men had a tendency toward colorful language, but they did own several pets, and based on my experience with them, it seemed like they'd be good working with the animals we housed. We really just needed someone to be on-site in case of an emergency, or to tend to sick or injured animals we might house in the future. Tank and Gunner seemed like the type who wouldn't be squeamish about a less-than-pleasant job, should one arise, so they might work out if we could keep them away from the customers we dealt with during the day.

"Let's set up a time to talk to them," I decided. "Anyone else we should look at?"

"You can look through the files yourself if you'd like. There are other interested parties for the full-time position, but I felt Tiffany would be the best choice."

"Okay, I'll talk to her, and we can take it from there."

The fact that I had to put my truck into four-wheel drive to get out of the parking lot at the end of the day was absurd. Yes, Ashton Falls is in the mountains, and yes, our weather can be unpredictable, but to have close to two feet of snow fall in April was almost unheard of. Luckily, the main thoroughfares had been plowed, so once I got onto the highway the travel was relatively painless. In spite of the weather, it had been a good day. Jeremy and I had managed to get the pen we planned to use for the rescued bunnies cleaned in plenty of time to accept delivery of the sixty rather than the hundreds of animals we feared. Our veterinarian, Scott Walden, had looked them over and declared them fit for adoption, so we went ahead and posted an ad for an adoption clinic to be held the following weekend. I contacted the reporter who was interested in doing the story, and she was more than willing to advertise all of the services we provided, including bunny adoption, as part of her feature about the cubs.

I interviewed Tiffany and found that Jeremy was correct in his assumption that she'd make a wonderful addition to our staff. She was bubbly and friendly, with an impressive background and a natural ease with the animals. I hired her on the spot, and Jeremy planned to begin training her this week. To add icing to the cake, I found the perfect doggy daddy for a hard-to-place greyhound with emotional issues that I was close to giving up hope for. By the time I stopped by the printers, the menus were ready and waiting. The printer and I chatted for a few minutes before Charlie and I headed over to the bank.

By the time I pulled into the lot, it had stated to snow. Again. Maybe Blakely *was* the real Jack Frost. The crazy weather seemed to indicate that something magical as well as sinister was in play. I knew that Blakely wouldn't appreciate my bringing Charlie indoors, but it was cold outside, and I feared the temperature in the truck would drop to an uncomfortable level for the little dog should Blakely engage me in a lengthy conversation, as he was prone to do. As I was helping him out of the truck, I noticed a figure scurrying away from the back of the building toward the wooded area behind the bank.

"Did you see that?" I asked Charlie, afraid that I was losing my mind.

Charlie barked.

Visibility was bad as the snow combined with the darkening sky made individual images difficult to decipher, but I could swear the figure I saw scampering away was none other than the Easter Bunny.

"I must have rabbits on the brain," I said, laughing at the absurdity of the real Easter Bunny leaving the bank. I had, after all, been processing rabbits all day and that, combined with the play, had most likely skewed my perception.

I tucked one of the menus into my jacket, picked Charlie up, and made my way to the back door of the bank. I reached for the buzzer just as I noticed that the door had been left ajar. The bunny must not have closed it when he fled. I stepped inside, hoping I wouldn't set off any alarms. I set Charlie down on the tile floor and removed my boots before making my way down a dark hallway toward Blakely's office. When I poked my head into his office door, it was empty.

"Mr. Blakely," I called. "It's Zoe Donovan. I'm here with the menu."

I listened, but there was no answer. The rest of the bank appeared to be dark, and I hesitated to wander around without knowing what, if any, security alarms might have been activated. I was preparing to leave a sample of the menus and a note for Blakely when

Charlie took off down the darkened hallway on his own.

"Charlie," I called.

He didn't respond, which was odd, because he usually came running at the sound of my voice.

"Charlie," I tried again, in a louder and sterner tone.

Charlie barked in the distance but refused to come. A knot formed in my stomach as I remembered the last time Charlie had refused to obey a direct command. An image sprang to mind that I quickly repressed. I didn't need to think about that as I made my way slowly down the dark hall.

"Charlie," I called again. "Get your furry butt back here this minute."

Again, my call was met with the sound of barking from some point beyond the hallway. I reached for my cell, only to remember that I'd left it sitting on the console of the truck. As I inched forward, I noticed a dim light in the distance. Once I made my way to the main section of the bank, security lights provided enough illumination for me to see the familiar shapes of the lobby and customer service counter. The lights were dim, so the figures within my line of vision appeared like vague images without color or texture. I hate to admit it, since I pride myself on my courage, but the eerie feeling of the empty bank caused chills to tingle up my spine.

"Charlie," I called again, praying that he'd come and I wouldn't have to continue into the darkness.

The sound of the return bark seemed to be coming from the area behind the counter, where I knew the safety deposit boxes and bank safe were located. I headed toward the open doorway, preparing to give Charlie a piece of my mind for ignoring my call, when I tripped and fell over something lying on the floor just outside of the doorway. I sat up and turned to look back toward the source of my tumble.

"Not again," I groaned, as I scooted away from it, stood up, and hurried back down the hall toward the phone in Blakely's office.

"I need you to describe the man you saw leaving the bank," Sheriff Salinger said an hour later.

"I told you," I snapped. "The Easter Bunny. Floppy ears, cottontail, big feet. I'm not sure what more I can tell you."

I knew I was being short with Salinger, who for once actually seemed to be trying to be nice, but to find another body . . . The odds, I knew, were beyond astronomical.

"How tall would you say he was?" Salinger tried again.

"I don't know. It was getting dark and snowing, and the figure was running away from me. The man had a fake head on, so it's really hard to say, but if I had to guess, I'd say over six feet."

"Would you say that the costume the man wore is the same one you're using for the play?"

I thought about it. It really had been hard to make out any details in the dark. "I don't know. Maybe. It was too dark to really differentiate colors, but the costume was definitely similar."

"And your grandfather, Luke Donovan, is playing the Easter Bunny in the play and is currently in possession of the costume?"

"You aren't seriously suggesting that my Pappy did this?"

"I have to explore all possibilities," Salinger reminded me.

"Pappy didn't do it. He's playing the Easter Bunny in the play, but I'm pretty sure he doesn't have the costume at his house. Blakely insisted on wearing his costume to *every* rehearsal, but the remainder of the cast won't actually wear costumes until the week before the performance. The last I saw of Pappy's bunny costume, Gilda had sent it out for alterations, so I guess you can check with her."

"Can you think of anyone who might have had motive to kill Blakely?" Salinger asked the standard question.

"Sure. Pretty much everyone in town. The guy was a real tool."

"Zoe," Salinger said, looking directly at me, "I know you're upset, but I really need you to focus. It's entirely possible that something you saw could end up making the difference in whether or not we track down the killer."

I took a deep breath. "I know. I'm sorry. What do you want to know?"

"Did you see or hear anything unusual when you entered the bank?"

I thought about it. "Not really. The door was open, which was odd. I was supposed to buzz Blakely when I got here with the menus, and he was going to open the door for me. I suppose it's possible the killer buzzed him and Blakely opened the door assuming it was me."

"Your theory makes sense to a point, but for that to be the case, the killer would have had to know that Blakely was going to be staying late and that he was expecting someone. Other than yourself and Ellie, did anyone know your plans to stop by?"

"My assistant, Jeremy, took the message in the first place, but other than that, I didn't mention it to anyone."

"I know that you're involved in the same play Mr. Blakely was going to appear in. Other than rehearsals, have you had any contact with the victim in recent weeks?"

"Yeah," I answered. "Some. I do my banking here, and he's been *very* involved with the loan he gave to Ellie for her eatery."

"And how has he seemed during business hours?"

"Obsessive, compulsive, controlling, irritating. Totally normal."

"I had some of my men follow what was left of the footprints left in the snow. There was a single set of large prints that could very well have come from prop shoes going from the rear door of the bank, across the meadow, and into the edge of the forested area behind the building. Once the prints disappeared into the forest, the large prints were mixed in with numerous others going in every direction. It's possible there were originally several other sets, but snow tends to drift in the meadow, so any footprints made earlier might have been covered up, while the ones under the trees on the other side of the meadow would have been protected. Did you see anyone other than the Easter Bunny when you first arrived?"

I thought about it. "No. I just saw the one figure."

"Did you hear anything that might help us? A vehicle? A snowmobile? Anything at all?"

"No, nothing. Although a vehicle or snowmobile would have left tracks. Where did the prints lead?"

"Everywhere and nowhere. It appears that someone ran around making prints in every direction to confuse us. So far, none of the prints appear to lead to tire tracks of any type. We plan to keep looking, but with the heavy snowfall, the tracks are disappearing quickly."

"It sounds like you have your work cut out for you. Are Zak and Charlie still here?"

We had been conducting our interview in one of the offices in the admin section of the bank, but I knew that Zak had shown up shortly after I called him and had taken possession of Charlie.

"They're in the lobby."

"So can I go? It really has been a long day and I'm exhausted."

Salinger looked at me with what could only be interpreted as sympathy. "You can go, but if I have further questions . . ."

"You know where to find me."

"Are you sure I can't make you something to eat?" Zak asked after he'd driven Charlie and me back to the boathouse and poured me a glass of wine.

"No thanks," I answered. "Did you get hold of Pappy?" I realized that I should give him a heads up about who had appeared to kill Blakely and how that might make him a suspect.

"I did. He was with your dad and mom, helping put things away all day, so he has a solid alibi."

"And the costume?"

"He said it's tucked away safely in his closet. He ran home to check just to make sure."

I leaned my head back against the sofa and closed my eyes. I had to be dreaming. That was the only explanation that made sense. Maybe if I focused really hard, I could force myself to wake up from this bizarre nightmare. First there was Blakely's absurd behavior regarding Jack Frost, and then there was the delivery of dozens of bunnies, followed by Blakely's death by the Easter Bunny. If I wasn't dreaming, I decided, then I must have totally lost my mind. There was no way this could all be real.

I might have drifted off because the next thing I was aware of was the sensation of kisses on my cheek. Charlie kisses, not Zak kisses, but nice and comforting all the same. Charlie was very sensitive to my emotions and had barely left my side since we'd gotten home. I knew that my distress was upsetting him, so I opened my eyes and smiled at him.

Charlie laid his head on my lap and let me take comfort from his warm body. There had been so many times in the past when Charlie had provided a lifeline to sanity as my world seemed to be spinning out of control. I don't know what I would have done without him.

"That was Ellie on the phone," Zak informed me.

"The phone rang?"

"Like six times. It was on the table right next to you. Didn't you hear it?"

"No. I guess I must have dozed off. What did she want?"

"She called to ask about the menus, but after I explained why they weren't delivered, she insisted on coming over. I hope that's okay."

"Yeah, it's okay. Is Levi coming as well?"

"She was going to call him."

I sat up and took another sip of the very expensive wine Zak left a supply of at my boathouse. He says he wants me to have the finest things, but truth be told, I think he simply got tired of drinking my cheap stuff.

"I know your natural inclination is going to be to jump right into this, but I really think you should stay out of things this time," Zak cautioned. "I don't want you putting yourself in danger. Again."

"I know. You're right. I should stay out of it."

"So will you?" Zak looked uncertain.

"Probably not."

Zak sighed. "I don't know what I'm going to do with you."

"Oh, I have a few ideas." I grinned.

"As good as that sounds, Ellie will be here in a few minutes," Zak reminded me.

"Maybe, but we still have a few minutes."

Zak laughed. He sat down on the sofa and pulled me into his lap. He kissed me in such a way as to communicate both his love for the defects in my personality that caused me to become involved in things I had no business sticking my nose in *and* his concern for my safety. There are those of you who might wonder how I can interpret all of this from a single kiss, but suffice it to say that I know Zak, and I've come to be able to translate and understand what his heart longs to tell me.

"Hmm, hmm." Levi cleared his throat as he and Ellie walked through the front door of the boathouse.

"Don't you ever knock?" I complained as Zak ended his kiss.

"We did." Ellie grinned. "Several times."

"Oh." I blushed as I straightened my clothes and slid off Zak's lap and onto the sofa beside him.

"Can I get you some wine?" Zak offered.

Both Levi and Ellie accepted as they settled in front of the fire.

"You realize," Levi teased, "that you're never going to be able to shed your reputation as a dead-body magnet if you don't stop finding murder victims?"

"I don't find them; they find me."

"Maybe, but this time it could have been me." Ellie looked pale. "It should have been me. I haven't been able to think of anything else since I talked to Zak."

"It wouldn't have been you," I assured Ellie.

"What do you mean, it wouldn't have been me? I was the one who was supposed to meet Blakely. If I hadn't had to go to the county and hadn't asked you to take the menus to the bank for me, it would have been me who found him. I'm not as brave as you are. I would have been a total basket case by this point."

"If you'd arrived at the bank and Blakely wasn't in his office, what would you have done?" I asked.

"I would have left a menu on his desk and left."

"Exactly. It wouldn't have been you who found the body because you wouldn't have gone looking for him."

"I see your point." Ellie looked relieved.

"It would most likely have been some poor teller who showed up first for work tomorrow morning," Levi speculated.

"So what happened?" Ellie asked. "Do they have any suspects?"

I filled Levi and Ellie in on everything I knew, from the presence of the Easter Bunny to the location of the body.

"If the security-room door was open, it had to have been a robbery," Ellie said. "Someone must have buzzed Blakely, forced his way in through the back door once he opened it, strong-armed Blakely into opening the security room, and then killed him once he gained access."

"Your theory makes sense to a point. I had a similar idea myself, but Salinger pointed out that for the thief to have taken advantage of the fact that Blakely was expecting me to buzz him, the thief would have had to know that I was planning to come by. The only one who knew the plan other than you and me was Jeremy, unless you mentioned it to someone."

"The printer knew that you were going to deliver the menus to the bank after you picked them up," Ellie informed me. "I suppose he could have mentioned it to someone or might even have said something about it while other people were in the shop."

"Good point. I suppose I should suggest that Salinger talk to the guy."

"Or maybe Blakely was meeting someone else," Levi guessed. "Someone in addition to Ellie. It's possible Blakely knew and was expecting his killer."

"Perhaps," I acknowledged.

"Are you going to investigate?" Ellie asked.

I looked at Zak. "As of yet I'm undecided."

"It's not like you really cared about the victim or someone you care about is a suspect," Ellie pointed out. "Maybe you *should* let Salinger handle it."

"If you *were* going to investigate," Levi prodded, "who would you put on the suspect list?"

I thought about it. Blakely wasn't a popular man. There were a lot of people in town who had issues about the way he conducted business. It wasn't that he was dishonest; it was more that he was ruthless in his quest to get exactly what he wanted.

"Gilda was pretty annoyed with him for ruining her play," Ellie offered. "As if the rewrite wasn't bad enough, the addition of that ridiculous costume was mortifying. Gilda even mentioned canceling the play if she couldn't talk Blakely out of his tights."

Levi laughed. "Now I'll be stuck with the image of Gilda talking Blakely out of his tights."

"I guess that didn't come out right." Ellie blushed.

"I doubt Gilda would kill the man," Zak pointed out.

"Oh, I don't know. She was awfully mad," Ellie insisted.

"I heard Frank Valdez had to take out a loan to deal with Michael's legal bills, and Blakely insisted on him using his house as collateral. I guess things have been tough, and Blakely was threatening to foreclose," Levi offered.

Frank's son, Michael, had been involved in a messy murder investigation over Halloween the year before that had cost the family a lot of money they really didn't have. What Levi said seemed to confirm the rumor I'd heard about the reason Frank had backed out of the play when Blakely came on board.

"Ernie Young said he owed Blakely money as well," I contributed, mentioning the owner of the local market. "He was worried that Blakely would pull something like he did on Ellie if he tried to renegotiate the loan, but he was in a tough spot."

"Which I suppose makes Ernie and me both suspects," Ellie pointed out.

"That's it." Levi clapped his hands together. "Ellie did it. Case closed; let's get pizza."

"I didn't do it." Ellie threw a sofa pillow at Levi's head. "I might have thought about it a time or two, though. I've never met anyone quite as OCD as Blakely. Do you know, he had to approve the color paint I used on the walls, as well as the brand and size of microwave I chose?"

"Let's face it, the suspect list on this one is going to be long," Zak contributed. "Maybe we should just let Salinger do his thing so we can get on with our lives."

"Yeah," I had to agree. "You're right. This investigation is going to be long and complicated, and the last thing I need is more complications in my life." I felt good that I'd made a logical rather than an emotional decision. Maybe Zak's steady nature was finally rubbing off on me.

Chapter 4

Friday, April 11

When I agreed to let Salinger handle things, I'd been fairly certain that I'd be able to do just that, but by the time the following Friday rolled around, I was less certain. A lot had changed over the course of the week. For one thing, Salinger had been running around town accusing practically everyone who'd done business with Blakely of killing him. It seemed that everywhere I went, people were angry and tensions were high. It occurred to me that Salinger had no idea how to run an investigation. In a few short days, he had everyone suspecting everyone else. If it were me investigating possible suspects, I'd do so with a lot more tact so as to gain the information I needed without making people feel they were being accused of such a heinous crime.

On a positive note, without Blakely's interference, Ellie was able to go ahead with her opening, which was scheduled for today. The storm and cold spell that had hit the area had cleared, making way for sunshine and temperatures in the midsixties. I couldn't believe I was actually dressing for the opening in a flirty sundress and strappy sandals.

"Wow, you look nice," Zak commented as I opened the door of the boathouse to greet him.

"Thanks." I twirled around in a circle. "It's new."

"And short. Maybe we should skip the opening."

"Not on your life." I reached for my sweater. "We're already late, so we need to hurry."

"Did you get a hold of your mom?" Zak asked as he kissed me on the cheek to avoid messing up my lipstick, a concession I'd made to the spring fever that had suddenly hit me, bringing out my seldom-seen girlie side.

"Yeah. She has a doctor appointment. Dad is going to take her and then they're going to meet us at Ellie's Beach Hut. Pappy's covering the store, so Dad has the entire day off."

"Is Ellie nervous?"

"Totally. Levi got a sub for his classes so he could help her get set up. Rob offered to help as well, so I'm not sure how that's all going to work out, but hopefully everyone will behave so Ellie won't be stressed out more than she already is."

"Rob seems like a nice guy." Zak helped me on with my sweater. "I'm not sure why Levi doesn't like him."

"He's jealous."

"Of Ellie? I thought they were just friends."

I looked at Zak like he'd lost his mind. "Where exactly have you been?"

"Apparently wallowing around in the dark. Anything else I should know about?"

"Probably." I told Charlie to stay as Zak and I exited the boathouse. I stopped for a moment to soak up the feel of the sun on my face. "Isn't it glorious? It felt like spring was never going to get here this year."

"It is a beautiful day," Zak agreed. "Maybe we can take the boat out later."

"Sounds nice, but I really should help Jeremy get ready for the bunny adoption. We've had quite a few inquiries, so we got a permit to hold it in the community center. I think we should have a good turnout."

"I thought the community center was being used for the play."

"Gilda decided to cancel rehearsals until next week so she can rework the script now that we don't have a Jack Frost. To be honest, I'm relieved she didn't simply try to replace Blakely and keep the play as written. The story never did come together. I think Gilda is thinking of using a less complex script, followed by something fun for the kids, like an egg hunt. There's even talk of doing the play outdoors. If the new script doesn't require much in the way of sets, we can use the gazebo in the park as the stage and have people bring blankets to sit on. Weather permitting, of course."

"I bet Pappy was relieved that the Jack Frost plot had to be rewritten," Zak commented.

"You have no idea. I thought he was going to run screaming from the community center the first time Blakely showed up in his Jack Frost getup."

The reality was that the entire cast was relieved that Blakely was out of the picture. I had to wonder whether someone involved in the play was responsible for the man's death.

"Speaking of Blakely, I guess you heard they arrested Doug Barton."

"Doug?" I frowned. "Why would they arrest Doug?"

Doug was an ex-employee of the bank who'd left under less than ideal circumstances several months earlier, but he'd always seemed like a nice guy and I couldn't imagine him hurting a flea, little alone killing a man. Of course, pretty much every suspect who had come to mind was a friend or neighbor I'd eliminated for the same reason.

"Salinger found e-mails Doug had written to Blakely accusing him of ruining his life. It seems his wife left him after he was fired, taking their two-year-old twins with her."

"And?" I asked.

"And what?"

"I'm sure Salinger must have more than the e-mails if he's going to accuse the guy of such an atrocious crime."

"I'm sure he does, but I'm afraid I'm not privy to that information at this time."

"But you can get it."

"I'm sure I can, but if you're really interested, you might try just asking Salinger. He seems to be softening toward you."

"Yeah, maybe. I doubt Doug is guilty, but I can see why Salinger is anxious to arrest someone. I'm afraid his clumsy interrogation methods have the entire town up in arms. If he doesn't close the case soon, his may be the next murder we have to investigate."

"Yeah." Zak turned onto the beach road, where the pier was located. "I talked to Ernie Young and he was livid at the way he was treated. He was even talking about petitioning the county for a replacement."

"If Doug isn't guilty, maybe we should help Salinger," I suggested.

"I thought you disliked the guy. I thought you'd be happy to see Salinger replaced."

"I'll admit he isn't my favorite person, but based on the rumors I've heard, it seems like half the town is ready to lynch him. I just thought we could help focus him a bit."

"Do you think he'd welcome our help?" Zak asked.

I thought about it. "I think he just might. Let's face it, he's over his head with this one."

"And you think you could do better?"

"I know *we* could do better. Oh look, there's a parking space near the front."

"It looks like a good turnout," Zak commented as we pulled into the parking area that served both the pier and the beach. I could see that parking was going to be an issue during the summer, when the beach was packed almost every day.

"I can't believe the snow has completely melted off the beach. It looks like a summer day."

"It's been in the sixties all week," Zak pointed out. "And the beach has sun for most of the day, so it doesn't take long."

"I really meant to get here earlier to help Ellie," I admitted. "I hope she isn't overwhelmed by the crowd."

"It looks like she had help." Zak nodded toward the outdoor seating area, where both Levi and Rob, as well as several other community members, were waiting tables.

"I don't see my dad's truck. I thought they might be here by now."

"Your mom seemed really tired the last time we saw them. Maybe they decided to skip it," Zak suggested.

"Maybe." I pulled my phone out of my purse, but there were no messages. "I should call them before we get swept up in the crowd."

I looked out toward the glassy lake as I waited for my dad to answer. A romantic ride in Zak's boat wasn't such a bad idea after all. I had a new bikini I was waiting to try out, and it was never too early to start working on my tan.

"Zoe," my dad answered. "I was just about to call you. I'm afraid we're going to miss the opening. We're at the hospital."

"Hospital? Is everything okay?"

"Your mom's blood pressure was a little high, and the doctor thought it was best that she be monitored for the time being. I'm sure she'll be fine, but Dr. Westlake wanted to be sure it wasn't going to turn into more of a problem."

"Should I come?"

"No, I don't think that's necessary. Your mother is resting comfortably and the baby seems to be fine. I'm sure Dr. Westlake is just being cautious. Enjoy the opening and give Ellie our love."

"Okay." I couldn't help but be worried. "I'll call you later. If they decide to keep her overnight, I'll come by."

"I'm sure your mother would like that."

"Everything okay?" Zak asked when I hung up.

"High blood pressure."

"Can we do anything?"

"Dad says no."

"Okay then, let's go congratulate Ellie on what looks like it's going to be a huge success."

"So how was your mom?" Jeremy asked the minute I walked through the front door of the Zoo later that afternoon. I'd called to let him know I was going to be later than I'd planned since, in spite of

Dad's assurances, I'd wanted to see for myself that Mom and Harper were okay.

"She's fine. Her blood pressure was a little high, so they wanted to take a closer look. They plan to keep her overnight, but if things remain stable, they'll let her go home tomorrow. I think my dad plans to move into the main house, though, until the baby is born."

"Makes sense. I worry about Gina being all alone during these final few weeks, but so far she's refused to let me stay with her."

"How is she doing?"

Jeremy shrugged. He'd had a rough road with his ex since she'd agreed to have the baby if he paid all the expenses and raised her on his own. Gina was a model who was used to world travel and glamour, not swollen ankles and stretch marks.

"Only a few more weeks," I said encouragingly.

"The doctor thinks she might be early. Let's just say we're both rooting for that big time."

"I suppose at this point both Mom and Gina could have their babies at any time."

"Yeah. I suppose I should see about a crib."

"You don't have a crib?"

"Money's been tight. I've pretty much cleaned out the small savings I had to pay for Gina's medical bills, and being out of work after the county closed the shelter didn't help."

Suddenly I had the best idea.

"Sounds like what you need is some downtime to unwind. How about you come by the boathouse for dinner with the gang and me tomorrow after the adoption clinic?"

"Sounds like fun."

"We'll grill up some steaks and make some margaritas. It'll be great."

Now all I had to do was call Ellie and have her contact the rest of the single parents group, and then call Levi and have him get in touch with Jeremy's other friends and Zak, and have everyone shop for the impromptu baby shower I'd just decided to throw. No one ever said baby showers needed to be only for women.

"Is Tiffany here today?" I asked.

"She's in the back, exercising the dogs. Bobby is here as well. It seems like those two have hit it off," Jeremy replied.

"Wonderful. I guess I'll go say hi, and then we can go over the plans for tomorrow."

"I think we can leave Tiffany in charge of the Zoo while we're at the adoption," Jeremy suggested. "She's caught on really quickly and seems to know exactly what to do. If she has a problem or a question, she can always call us. We'll only be a few minutes away."

"Sounds like a good way to try her out on her own. I'll ask her about it."

"Cool."

Tiffany and Bobby were in the large fenced area where we let the dogs play when I made my way to the back of the building. Bobby was tall and lanky, with dark hair that had a tendency to hang in his eyes. He seemed like a good kid who wasn't afraid to jump right into any job we might have for him, no matter how dirty or unpleasant it might be.

Tiffany was a young woman of average height who carried a bit of extra weight, though she certainly wasn't overweight. She had long brown hair, brown eyes, and an infectious smile. She seemed to *always* be in a fantastic mood, and her joy at every little thing was both welcome and infectious.

"Hi, guys," I greeted.

"Zoe, look what we taught Dolly to do." Bobby demonstrated as a lab mix we'd had for about a week jumped through the center of a Hula-Hoop when Bobby blew a whistle.

"Wow, that's awesome. We'll have to show off her new trick the next time we get someone in looking for a larger dog."

"I wish I could take her home, but Mom said no." Bobby sighed.

"One of the first things you'll learn is that there'll be many dogs and cats to whom you'll become attached, and you can't take them all home," I warned him. "It's one of the more difficult aspects of the job."

"Yeah, I guess, but as soon as I'm eighteen and can get my own place, I'm getting a dog."

"Unless the only apartment you can afford won't let you have a dog," Tiffany added.

"At least there are plenty here who need your love and attention, even if it's temporary," I said in an attempt to encourage my new assistants. "Jeremy and I will be busy all day tomorrow at the bunny adoption. I was hoping you felt ready to be in charge of the place and could cover for us," I said, directing my comment to Tiffany.

"Really?" She grinned. "I'd love to cover for you. And don't worry, I know what to do. You can count on me." She jumped up in the air and let out a little screech, as if she couldn't contain her joy at the thought of being given the responsibility.

"I can help," Bobby offered. "If that's okay?"

"I think it would help Tiffany a lot if you could come in. Can you both be here at eight and plan to work until closing? Jeremy or I will be by to help you lock up at the end of the day."

"Eight is perfect." Tiffany smiled.

"It should be a slow day. I have two adoptive doggy parents coming in to pick up their new family members. All of the paperwork has been completed and the dogs have been checked out by Scott and are ready to go. All you need to do is turn the dogs over to the customers and make sure they don't have any questions."

"Who's going to new homes?" Bobby asked.

"Jackie and Sunset."

"Awesome. They've both been waiting for quite a while."

"It can be harder to place larger dogs, but I think we managed to find them humans who will fit perfectly with their energy and temperament. I need to go help Jeremy with some forms for tomorrow, but stop by the desk before you leave so I can show you a few things you may need to know."

"We will," they both said in unison.

After I got off work, I headed over to Salinger's office, praying the entire way that he hadn't left for the day. I was less certain than Zak that the man would talk to me, but I had to try, if for no other reason than to assuage my curiosity. I had to admit that even I was surprised that I'd managed to stay out of things as long as I had. I suppose at least part of my ability to adhere to Zak's request to let Salinger handle things could be attributed to the fact that I'd been so busy that I'd barely had time to worry about a dead Jack Frost and a murderous Easter Bunny. Still, I didn't think I'd be able to let it go entirely until I was convinced the guilty party had been brought to justice.

"I was wondering how long it would take you to drop by," Salinger greeted me as I was escorted into his office.

"You were expecting me?" I asked innocently.

"Since the moment I arrested Doug Barton. I imagine you think I've made a mistake."

"Perhaps, but I don't have all the facts. I don't suppose you'd be willing to share your reasons for arresting Doug?"

"Actually, I do mind, but experience has taught me that if I don't tell you, you'll just dig around on your own, making my life miserable in the process."

I sat back and settled in. Zak was right. All I *did* need to do was ask.

"As you know, Doug was formerly employed by Ashton Falls Community Bank. He and Blakely had a falling out several months ago and Blakely fired him. Since then, Blakely received a series of e-mails from Doug accusing him of destroying his life. Apparently, his wife left him after he was fired, and he'd threatened retaliation of an unspecified nature on numerous occasions."

"Just because he threatened to do it doesn't mean he did," I pointed out.

"True, but security cameras show Doug entering the bank shortly before closing without showing him leaving."

"So you think he hid and waited until everyone left, then attacked Blakely?"

"That's my theory. Doug would know where to hide to avoid detection by the security staff as they locked up because he'd worked at the bank for several years."

"Speaking of cameras, wouldn't they show exactly who killed Blakely?" I realized.

"You'd think that would be the case, but unfortunately someone turned the cameras to the main part of the bank off after everyone left."

"You think Doug knew how to do that?"

"It would make sense that he did. He'd worked himself into the number-two position at the bank before he was fired. The only cameras that remained on were those in the security room, which are rigged to remain on at all times. We see the cameras go off at five and then there's nothing until we see Blakely enter the security room at five-twenty. He enters the room, then turns back toward the door. He yells something we haven't been able to make out as of yet, and then runs back toward the entrance of the room. There's the sound of a shot at that point. We assume he died instantly, because the body was found just outside the security-room door. It seems the only one who could have pulled this off is someone who was familiar with the layout of the bank as well as the security system."

"So you think the killer knew about the cameras?"

"It would seem so. The killer didn't seem concerned about being seen outside of the door to the security room but was careful not to cross the line where the cameras in the room took over. My money is on an employee or ex-employee, which brings us back to Doug."

"What about the bunny costume? Did Doug come into the bank dressed like a bunny?" I asked.

"No, he didn't," Salinger said. "Is it *possible*," he emphasized the word, "that the man you saw running away wasn't really dressed in a costume? It was dark and snowing, and the man had his back to you and was already away in the distance, according to your statement. Perhaps he had a hood on his head or some other outerwear that created the illusion of a costume."

"I suppose it's possible," I had to admit. "It was dark, and everything you've said is true, but I was so certain at the time."

"In my experience, eyewitness accounts of an event are sketchy under the best of circumstances. If you have ten witnesses to an occurrence, you'll most likely get ten differing accounts of what happened. I have good reason to suspect Doug and as of this point no other solid leads. If you have anything to contribute, this would be the time to do so."

"You want my opinion?"

"I asked for it, didn't I?"

At that moment, I was both proud and honored that in spite of our long and rocky relationship, Salinger was actually asking me what I thought. "To be honest," I answered, "it does sound like you have probable cause to arrest Doug, and I don't have a better suspect in mind. If I hear anything, I'll be sure to let you know."

Chapter 5

Saturday, April 12

"Who would have thought that there were so many people in the market for bunnies?" I commented to Jeremy the next afternoon, as we processed piles of adoption paperwork. My dad had managed to get us a killer deal on cages and rabbit food, so we were able to provide each adoptive family with everything they'd need to take their very own bunny home that day. We'd decided to bypass the much more complicated adoption process we normally employed in order to speed things up with the holiday just around the corner, after which there wouldn't be a kid in town left yearning for their very own Easter pet.

"I just hope we don't end up getting them all back the day after Easter," Jeremy said.

"Don't even think it."

"The adoption procedure we've developed over the years was the result of impulse adoptions followed by frequent returns," Jeremy reminded me.

"True, but bunnies are a lot lower maintenance than dogs and cats. We're providing the cage and food to get them started. What more could a prospective family want?"

"I'm really enjoying having Squeaky for a pet. Hamsters are fun *and* easy."

"Maybe Squeaky wants a bunny roommate?"

"Hardly. I'm pretty sure he likes being an only pet. That way he doesn't have to share the attention."

"Do you have any bunnies that are all white?" An adorable little girl with long blond pigtails wearing a bright yellow dress asked.

"We might have one or two left. Are your parents here?"

"My mom is parking the car. She said she'd meet me inside."

"Okay." I walked around the table I was sitting behind. "Let's see what we can find."

I took the girl by the hand and led her to the area where we were keeping the bunnies that hadn't been adopted yet.

"I want one named Annabelle," the girl informed me. "She's going to stay in my room and I'm going to take care of her all by myself."

"Do you know how to take care of a bunny?" The girl couldn't be more than five years old.

"You have to give her water and keep the cage clean," the girl answered.

"And don't forget to feed her," I added.

"Lettuce and carrots."

"These are the bunnies we have left." I walked up and down the row of bunnies. Many of them were multicolored, but there was a white one with a single black spot circling one eye. "This is one of our smallest females." I opened the cage and took the bunny out. "She's not *all* white, but she's mostly white. Do you want to hold her?"

The girl nervously held out her arms. I'd handled this particular rabbit on several occasions and knew she was not only small but mellow as well.

"So what do you think?" I asked.

"Did her daddy hit her in the eye?"

"No." I smiled. "Her eye isn't black because it's hurt, it's just a marking she was born with."

"Is her name Annabelle?"

"You know, I think it is."

"So who do we have here?" A woman, I assumed the girl's mother, walked up behind us as we talked. Like her daughter, she had long blond hair and large blue eyes framed by dark lashes.

"This is Annabelle," the girl answered. "She has a black eye, but her daddy didn't hit her."

The mother looked surprised at the girl's statement. I had a feeling the sweet child holding Annabelle might have been the victim of her dad's temper on at least one occasion.

"She's really beautiful." The mother knelt down so that she was on eye level with her daughter. "And she's really small as well. Just your size."

"Can I keep her?" The girl smiled hopefully.

The mom looked up at me. "I'm afraid we don't have a lot of money, but my daughter really wants a pet to sleep in her room with her. We just moved to the area and Rosalie is still trying to adjust to her new circumstances. We can't have dogs or cats in our apartment, so when I saw your sign announcing bunnies for adoption, I hoped that could be the answer I was praying for."

"I'm sure we can work something out. How about we put Annabelle back in her cage so your mom can fill out the paperwork? Maybe your dad can load the cage into your car."

"My daddy is in jail," the girl stated.

"Oh, I'm sorry." Talk about inserting your foot in your mouth. "Maybe Jeremy can load the cage while we do the paperwork."

I felt bad for both the mom, who hurried through the paperwork and seemed anxious to get out of there, and the little girl, who knew that sometimes black eyes came from dads. I told the woman that she could have the bunny for free, gave her a month's worth of food and rabbit litter, and told her that if she needed anything, she should come by the Zoo.

"Thank you." The woman had tears in her eyes. "Things have been hard lately, and I think this sweet bunny might really cheer Rosalie up."

"I'm happy to know that Annabelle has a good home with a little girl who loves her." I watched the woman and child walk away. The little girl was so happy that she twirled her way all the way to the car.

"Cute kid," Jeremy commented as he returned from loading Annabelle.

"I know you meant hot mom," I teased. Rosalie's mother was blond and petite, exactly Jeremy's type. I picked up the adoption paperwork and looked at it. "The daughter's name is Rosalie and Mom's name is Jessica Anderson. They just recently moved to town, and it looks like she lives in your apartment building."

"They must be the new folks in 4B."

"Maybe you can check to see how Annabelle is doing in a day or two," I suggested. "I got the idea there's been a lot of turmoil in the family as of late, and they'd probably welcome a friendly neighbor."

"I'll do that. Maybe Rosalie would like to meet Squeaky."

"I'm sure she would, and Jessica might benefit from the single parents group. I think the dad is out of the picture."

"You know me, always willing to do a good deed." Jeremy grinned.

"Yeah, I'll bet." I was certain his enthusiasm had more to do with Rosalie's cute mom than anything else.

"So are we still on for tonight?" Jeremy asked.

"Six-thirty, and don't be late," I confirmed.

"That'll give me time to drop the unadopted bunnies at the Zoo, check in with Tiffany, then head home for a quick shower. Can I bring anything?"

"No. Zak is barbecuing, Ellie is bringing a salad, and Levi is bringing dessert. I think we have everything else we need."

"I feel bad not contributing."

"Don't worry about it. The next time the gang hangs out, you can bring the dessert."

"Deal."

"What time did you tell Jeremy to be here?" Ellie asked me later that evening.

"Six-thirty," I replied. I looked around the crowded room, realizing I had no idea Jeremy had so many friends. "I guess it's a good thing we decided to move this to Zak's. There's no way all these people would have fit in my little boathouse."

"Once I notified the people in the single parents group about our plan to throw Jeremy a baby shower, they all had additional suggestions, and before we knew it, we had a mob. It looks like Jeremy won't have to buy a single thing for Morgan, although he may have to move into a bigger apartment to fit in all this stuff. By the way, how did the bunny adoption go?"

"Really well. We placed all but eight of the cute little buggers. I'm hoping we can get people to come in to adopt their own furry bundles of joy over the next few weeks."

"They are cute. And a lot lower maintenance than a dog or cat. Jeremy should think about keeping one for Morgan."

"Jeremy has Squeaky," I reminded Ellie about the hamster he'd adopted in February.

"Oh, yeah, I forgot. Is Squeaky still working out okay?"

"Jeremy seems to *love* him," I confirmed. "I have the feeling that little guy has a big heart to go with his playful and mischievous nature. He's the perfect pet for both Jeremy and Morgan."

"It was nice of Zak to buy all the food for the party. The steaks alone probably cost more than I make in a month."

"You know Zak. He's always happy to help out, and I think he's enjoying playing host. He even opened the roof of the pool area. Luckily, he has a bunch of swim trunks to lend. There are about twenty guys involved in a very serious water polo game."

Ellie looked out of the window. "It's Jeremy. Tell everyone to come into the living room."

I went to fetch the masses while Ellie went out to the driveway to stall Jeremy. We'd parked the majority of the cars at the boathouse and shuttled people over so as not to tip off the expectant father. When Jeremy walked through the front door and everyone yelled surprise, I really thought he was going to cry. Perhaps a surprise party hadn't been the best idea after all.

"Scotch," I said, handing Jeremy a drink.

"I can't believe you did all this." He hugged Ellie and me.

"We all pitched in," I told him.

"This is so . . . it's just that I never expected . . . there must be fifty people here."

"Probably more than that; I was unsuccessful in getting the gang in the pool out to greet you."

"And the gifts." He looked toward the side of the room where I'd set everything out rather than asking him to open them. "I bet I won't have to buy a single thing."

"That's the plan."

Jeremy hugged me again. "How can I ever thank you?"

"Trust me, you thank me every day. I couldn't do what I do at the Zoo without you and was happy for the chance to repay you. Now go. Mingle. There are appetizers on the table, Zak has steaks on the grill, and there's a bar set up near the pool."

"Poor Jeremy. I think he was on the verge of tears," Ellie commented after he'd wandered away.

"Yeah, he was really surprised."

"Jeremy is a good guy. He's going to make a great dad."

"I haven't seen Rob."

"He'll be a little late," Ellie informed me. "Hannah had a gymnastics class. They're coming by after."

"Gymnastics? Isn't she like one?"

"She just turned two, but I guess they start them young. At this point they really just let the kids play, but there are some kids in her group who are three and four and already on the balance beam."

"You're kidding."

"The beam is basically on the floor, but kids are very coordinated. I usually don't take kids into my dance classes until they're in kindergarten, but after attending Hannah's gym classes, I'm seriously thinking about adding something for three- and four-year-olds."

"Sounds like a nightmare." I cringed.

Ellie laughed. "Why? Kids are cute."

"And loud and messy, with the attention spans of gnats."

"Unlike animals, who are never loud and messy," Ellie pointed out.

"Good point. Still, I have a hard time imagining myself trying to teach a roomful of kids anything. In fact, I have a hard time imagining a roomful of kids. If I'm totally honest, I have a hard time imagining myself with one kid."

"You don't want kids?" Ellie asked.

"I don't know. Maybe someday, in the very distant future."

"Personally, I can't wait to have kids. Dating Rob and being with Hannah as she goes through the motions of her life has been wonderful."

"Sounds serious."

Ellie paused. "I guess. I know I'm serious about Hannah, but . . ."

"Just a bit less serious about Rob?" I guessed.

"I like Rob. He's kind and responsible. He loves Hannah and is such a good dad. We have common interests and have fun together."

"No fireworks?"

"Not even a sparkler."

"If you don't think you can love Rob, you should be careful about becoming too much of a mom to Hannah," I warned her. "You could both end up getting hurt."

"Yeah." Ellie sighed. "I've thought about that. I keep hoping the sparks will come once we get to know each other better, but so far not even a twinkle. Do you think sparks are really all that important in a long-term, committed relationship?" Ellie asked.

"Yeah, I do."

"I just wish I could find a guy who causes the sparks Levi does but is mature and committed, the way Rob is. Most days I can see myself having a very happy life with Rob, but then Hannah goes to bed and we settle in with a glass of wine in front of the fire and I find myself longing to go home to my own comfy bed. I guess the time has come to give this some serious thought."

"Speaking of that, here come Rob and Hannah now. Go have fun. There are extra swimsuits in the guest room, if you want to take Hannah swimming. I suppose she can just wear her diaper."

"That sounds like fun."

"Why the serious face?" Levi asked me after Ellie went off to greet Rob.

"Do you want kids?"

"Oh God, you're pregnant."

"No, I'm not pregnant."

"Ellie is pregnant." Levi paled.

"No, as far as I know Ellie isn't pregnant either. I was just curious whether you wanted kids. This is a baby shower, and babies *are* the main topic of conversation."

"No," Levi answered decisively. "I don't want kids."

"Ever?"

Levi paused. "I don't know. Ever is a long time, but I really can't imagine myself with kids. How about you? Do you want kids?"

"Not anytime soon."

"So why the intense look?"

I glanced at Ellie as she greeted Rob and picked up Hannah.

"Oh." Levi sighed. "Are they . . . did she mention . . . do you think they're getting serious?"

"Honestly, I don't know." I turned to face my friend. "What I do know is that Ellie wants kids. My bet is that she wants a bunch, and she wants them soon. If you aren't on the same page, you really need to move on to someone who is, even if she ends up single in the future. The two of you mean so much to me. I don't want either of you to get hurt."

"Yeah." Levi kissed the top of my head. "I hear you."

"Zoe!" Jeremy's best friend, Spike, came up from behind us and hugged me. Spike is the lead singer in the heavy metal band Jeremy plays with. I actually have no idea what his real name is; everyone calls him Spike because of the spikes in his hair, the dog collar he wears, and the various parts of his body, which are really uncomfortable-looking piercings. "Killer party."

"I'm glad you could come. I haven't seen you around much lately."

"Band had a gig. Jeremy had to drop out with all the hullabaloo with the twit and the kid, but I wanted to come by and show my support." Spike spoke with a really bad British accent that tended to flow between British, American, and something totally indefinable, but I was pretty sure he was born and raised in New Jersey.

"Well, I'm glad you were in town and could make it." I hadn't been aware that Jeremy had quit the band he'd been a part of ever since I'd known him, but they did travel quite a bit, so it made sense that he'd need to take a step back with the addition of a baby in his life.

"Been a bit of an upset since we've been gone," Spike commented.

"Upset?" I asked.

"Heard about the bloke who whacked the banker. Didn't figure him for a killer."

"Doug Barton?" Half the time Spike's tendency to speak in half sentences left me wondering exactly what he was talking about. "You know Doug Barton?"

"Did some business with the guy," Spike confirmed.

"What kind of business?" I found myself asking.

"Helped me invest a few pounds. Did a right nice job. Hate to see the guy rotting in a cell for something he didn't do."

"You think he's innocent?"

"Dude wasn't a bounder like his boss, although I guess he had a reason to whack the guy. Still, I don't figure he has the stones to do it. My money is on the neighbor."

"Neighbor?"

"Pansy with the lawsuit. Might want to check it out."

"Did you mention this to Salinger?" I wondered.

"Don't talk to coppers. Where is the loo in this pad?"

"Around the corner to the left."

I watched as Spike walked away. He really was a strange man, but Jeremy seemed to like him. I wasn't certain why he'd brought up the murder investigation to me, unless Jeremy had suggested he speak with me if he had information he wanted to share. He wasn't wrong in assuming that Salinger wouldn't give him the time of day. Maybe I'd ask Zak to do a little digging on the Internet to see if he could find out anything about this supposed lawsuit.

"That was some party," I said to Zak after only the two of us remained. We were sitting in the hot tub, sharing a bottle of champagne.

"Hmm," Zak agreed as he seared a trail of kisses across my neck.

"Do you want kids?"

Zak stopped kissing me and sat up straight. He looked me in the eye. "Kids?"

"Not now," I clarified.

Zak let out the breath he'd been holding.

"There was just a lot of baby talk tonight, and it hit me that a couple should be on the same page about something as important as kids. I almost feel like if the individuals who make up a couple aren't on the same page, they might be better off not pursuing the relationship in the first place."

"I see." Zak ran a finger across my cheek. "Yes, I'd like to have kids. Someday. How about you?"

I maneuvered myself so that I sat on Zak's lap facing him. I put my arms around his neck and looked him in the eye. "I think I might like to have *your* kids. Someday."

"So we're on the same page?"

"We are."

"Thank God." Zak locked his lips with mine and tightened his arms around me as we slid down into the bubbling water.

Chapter 6

Sunday, April 13

"Wake up, sleepyhead." Zak kissed me awake.

"What time is it?" I groaned.

"Almost noon."

I opened one eye and then closed it against the lightness of the room. "It's so bright."

"It's the middle of the day," Zak teased.

"Just another hour," I begged.

"I have breakfast," Zak bribed. "Hot coffee," he waved it under my nose, "strawberry crepes just the way you like them, with sour cream."

I leaned onto my elbows. "You made crepes?"

"I did."

Zak handed me the coffee and I took a sip. Talk about heaven.

"Put some clothes on and we'll eat on the deck. It's a beautiful day."

"Or we could eat in bed," I suggested seductively.

"We could." Zak kissed the tip of my nose. "But we have a lead and we need to be in town in just over an hour."

"A lead?"

"The case you bribed me into working on sometime after the chat about babies but before the second bottle of champagne."

"You have a lead? Already?"

"I've been up for hours. Now get dressed before your breakfast gets cold."

I quickly put on shorts, a tank top, and a sweatshirt. Then I pulled my long, curly hair into a ponytail and hurried downstairs, where Zak had crepes, sausages, coffee, and orange juice arranged nicely on the outdoor patio set. It really was a beautiful day. Charlie and Lambda were napping on the natural stone patio as the glassy lake just beyond the white-sand beach reflected the warm sun. I slipped off my sweatshirt as I sat down at the table. The sun on my shoulders felt like heaven after the long, long winter.

I shoveled the first of the four crepes Zak had made for me into my mouth before I paused for air. "These are so good. Tell me again why I don't let you make me breakfast every day."

"Fear of commitment and a desire to maintain your autonomy and take things slowly," Zak reminded me.

"Oh, yeah. So about this lead . . ."

"After I got back from my jog this morning, I looked into the lawsuit Spike mentioned. It seems that Blakely's neighbor, Truman Washington, was being sued by Blakely for an issue concerning the property line. It sounded like things had gotten ugly, so I did a little investigation while you were sleeping. Apparently, the person who built Washington's million-dollar house made an error when he calculated the exact borders of the property. Blakely didn't realize the mistake either, until he applied for a permit to build a pool house last summer and had the land surveyed. When the surveyor's report disclosed that the neighbor's house had been built four feet over the property line, Blakely demanded that the part of the structure on his property be demolished. It seems Washington offered to buy the sliver of land from Blakely, but he refused and instead took Washington to court, not only demanding that the house be removed from his property but that Washington pay him for the use of the land for the past six years."

"The house was built six years ago and this is just coming out?"

"It might never have come out if Blakely hadn't decided to expand."

"So what happened?"

"The case is still in court and has cost both men tens of thousands of dollars. I don't know if Washington was mad enough to kill over it, but those in the room at the time the story was told seemed to think he might be."

"Can't Washington take action against the contractor who made the original mistake?"

"He died several years ago and his business was dissolved."

"So do we follow up on this like Spike seemed to want me to?" I asked.

"I don't know. What do you think? Do you think Doug is guilty? Because if he is, we'd be wasting our time tracking down other leads."

I thought about it. Salinger had made some good points both about Doug's motive and his ability to pull off the act, but it bothered me just a bit that everything was coming together so easily. Doug was an obvious suspect, which in my book actually made it less likely that he was guilty.

"I'm not quite as certain as Salinger," I admitted. "And my guess is that Salinger is sitting in his office with his feet up on his desk, celebrating another closed case. I guess after I finish this delicious breakfast we should go have a chat with Washington. It can't hurt to see what he has to say."

"I thought you might say that, so I took the liberty of making an appointment with him, and also with the neighbors on either side of both men. I told them that I was creating a custom home-security system for a celebrity with a property similar to theirs and wondered if I might speak to them about what they liked and didn't like about the systems they currently have. We'll have to find a way to work in what we really want to talk about."

Our first stop was at Truman Washington's. He lived in a two-story house perched on the edge of a beautiful yet busy beach. My boathouse might be a tenth of the size, but I'd take the isolation of my little cove over Truman's expansive estate any day of the week. A glance at the area that I assumed was the disputed land was blocked off with yellow caution tape. Four feet might not sound like a lot, but I could see that a good part of the structure would need to be torn down to accommodate the property line, as well as the set back. Depending on load-bearing walls and whatnot, the project could run into the hundreds of thousands of dollars, as well as a whole lot of hassle and heartache.

"Mr. Washington," Zak greeted as the door was opened. "I'm Zak Zimmerman, and this is my friend, Zoe."

"I know who you are." The man shook Zak's hand. "Your reputation as a software genius precedes you."

"I appreciate your taking the time to answer a few questions."

"No problem at all. Come on in."

The house wasn't at all my style, but I'm sure to most it was breathtaking. Huge chandeliers hung from tall ceilings that created a feeling of spaciousness in spite of the dark, hardwood floors. The decoration was in a style I think of as upper-class snob, with sharp edges and harsh lines everywhere, but I had to admit that the open floor plan and huge rooms created an enviable space. Still, I'd take my comfy sofa with cushions you can sink into over Washington's designer sofa, which looked as if it had never been sat on.

"Your home is beautiful," I commented politely.

"Thank you. This place is my baby. I handpicked every piece of granite for the countertops and molding for the trim. The furnishings are all imported and every piece was chosen to complement the mood of each room."

"It's lovely," I lied.

"Perhaps we can sit on the deck while we chat. It's such a beautiful day."

"Sounds perfect."

Zak and I followed Washington out onto the huge deck. He really did have a fantastic view. The houses along this portion of the lake are situated along a busy stretch of beach, but the view of the water and the surrounding mountains is lovely all the same. I preferred my own secluded cove over Washington's location on the south shore, but I suppose if you're into people watching, the south shore is the place to be.

"It looks like you're doing an expansion," I said innocently as we passed near the surveyor's stakes.

"Not an expansion, I'm afraid." Washington launched into a heated retelling of the legal battle in which he'd been engaged with his neighbor. "Blakely was perfectly content with the property lines until he realized a mistake had been made. My attorney thought an offer to purchase the property would be an easy solution, but ol' Blakely was having nothing to do with a peaceful or easy fix. He didn't seem to care one bit about what his demands would do to my home. All he seemed to be interested in was making my life miserable. His lot is huge, and his house is set well to the other side. The four feet in question don't impact him at all. He said he might use it to put in some shrubs. Can you imagine? The man was going to require me to tear down my house so he could plant shrubs."

I looked across to Blakely's home and landscaping. I thought Washington was correct in his assessment that Blakely wouldn't miss the land he didn't even know he'd had in the first place.

"I've burned through so much money trying to fight his demands that I was beginning to lose hope that I'd be able to outlast him. Even if I would have won in the end, I wouldn't have had the resources left to actually buy him out."

"And now, with his death?"

"His daughter is the heir to his estate. My attorney has been in contact with hers, and he assures me that she's more than happy to have the property lines officially redrawn in exchange for fair-market value of the disputed property. I don't know who killed the guy, but I sure would like to thank them."

"I wasn't aware that Blakely had a daughter." As far as I knew, the man wasn't married.

"She's the product of a long-ago love affair and lives out of the area. I doubt she's ever even seen the house she inherited. She plans to sell it as soon as she can work out the legalities."

The conversation turned to home-security systems, giving me a chance to observe Washington while Zak questioned him. He seemed to have an excellent motive to kill Blakely, but as the men discussed early warning systems and alarm choices, Washington mentioned that he'd just returned two days earlier from a month-long trip to Palm Springs, giving him an air-tight alibi. Still, there was something about the man that gave me pause. He might not have killed Blakely, but I had the feeling that he wasn't being entirely honest with us either.

Our next appointment was with the neighbor to Blakely's right. As with all the homes in the neighborhood, it was large and beautiful, but with more of a mountain theme and less chrome, stone, and crystal. The man Zak had arranged to meet was someone with whom I'd been in contact when he adopted a dog from me the previous summer. I'd never been to his house, but I'd spoken to him on several occasions at the shelter, and he seemed like a nice guy who appeared to be much easier to get along with than either of his neighbors.

"Zoe, it's so good to see you," he greeted me.

"It's good to see you, too, Mr. Ellery. How's Goldie?"

"She's just fine. I'm sure she'd love to say hi. She's in the back with the grandkids, if you want to go on back while your guy and I chat."

I looked at Zak. I *would* like to say hi to Goldie, and I didn't want to do anything that might seem odd, but I also wanted to be present for whatever discussion the two men might have.

"Go on out and we'll meet you on the patio after we have our tour," Zak encouraged.

"Okay, I'll see you out there."

Goldie was a small golden retriever who made an excellent pet for the elderly man and his young grandchildren. I hadn't seen her since she'd been adopted, so she almost jumped into my arms when I entered the backyard.

"Boy, she really likes you," an adorable little girl with long brown ringlets said.

"That's because I'm the one who found her a wonderful home with your grandpa."

"My name is Julia. What's your name?"

"Zoe."

"Do you want to play hide and seek with us?"

"Sure, what are the rules?" The child was so adorable, I was willing to bet that people rarely said no to her.

"The boundaries are all the way from that fence," she pointed to a fence on the far side of her grandfather's property, "to the edge of the tape," she indicated the far side of Blakely's yard, where it met Washington's estate. "You hide and whoever is it has to find you."

"Are you sure it's okay to go into Mr. Blakely's yard?"

"Yeah. Grandpa says the old coot is dead and won't yell at us."

I had to smile at the child's use of the term.

"Did he used to yell at you?" I wondered.

"All the time."

"And you don't think the new owner will mind?"

"She said it was okay, as long as we stayed away from the pool."

"You spoke to her?" I asked.

"Yeah. Her name is Megan. She's nice, not like her dad."

Truman Washington had indicated that Blakely's daughter had most likely never seen the house. Why would he lie?

"Is she there now?"

"No, she was there, but she left a few days ago. She said she had to go to her other house."

"How long did she visit before she left?" I fished.

Julia seemed to be giving it quite a bit of thought. "I'm not sure, but she was here for my birthday, which is on March 6. She gave me a princess castle that fits most of my dolls."

"I see you've met Julia," Mr. Ellery said as he walked up behind us, with Zak in tow.

"She was just telling me about her awesome princess castle."

"Thing's as big as her room," Mr. Ellery reported. "Had to move it to one of the guest rooms, but she loves it."

"Do you want to see it?" Julia asked.

"Sure, I'd love to."

Unlike Washington's home, which featured cold and sharp surfaces, Mr. Ellery's was warm and inviting, with a pleasant color scheme and furniture you could actually sit on. Julia's bedroom gave evidence to the fact that her grandfather spoiled her quite lavishly. Not only did she have a princess castle in the spare room adjoining hers, but she had princess everything in her bedroom, including what had to amount to hundreds of dolls. The canopy bed that sat in the center of the room was painted an antique white and was piled high with pink and purple pillows and dozens of stuffed animals in every shape and size. As

I followed Julia as she introduced me to every one of her dolls, I couldn't help but wonder if I might have a little girl of my own someday. I tried to picture what she might look like and wondered if she'd be a girlie girl, like Julia, or a tomboy, like I had been. The possibilities both terrified and intrigued me.

"So?" I asked after Zak and I had said our good-byes and returned to the truck. Our next appointment was with the neighbor on the other side of Truman Washington's house, but we still had a few minutes.

Zak shrugged. "Ellery seemed open and more than willing to chat. I didn't get the feeling that he was hiding anything, but he didn't say anything that might help us either. In fact, I got the feeling that he was deliberately steering the conversation away from the legal battle between Blakely and Washington. If you want my opinion, he didn't want to get in the middle of the dispute between the two men."

"Well, I learned something interesting from Julia. She told me that Blakely's daughter, Megan, gave her the princess house on her birthday, which was March 6. Megan came to Ashton Falls at some point prior to that and just left a few days ago. Washington indicated that Blakely's daughter had most likely never even seen his house. It seems like he must have lied."

"Not necessarily. Washington was in Palm Springs until two days ago, and he mentioned that he had been there since just after the first of the year. Julia indicated that Megan left a few days ago. She may have arrived after Washington left and left before Washington returned. He may not even be aware that she was here in his absence."

"Yeah, I guess that's true. So what's the name of neighbor number three?" I asked.

"Dirk Pendleton."

"*The* Dirk Pendleton?" Dirk Pendleton was a well-known actor, a multimillionaire who lived, I thought, in New York.

"Actually, this is Dirk Pendleton Junior, and the house is a vacation home, but he happened to be in residence when I called and was happy to talk, so I figured what the heck."

What the heck? Was he kidding? Dirk Pendleton was only the most sought-after heartthrob of a generation. He was probably close to my dad's age, but unlike my dad, who was beginning to show his age, Dirk Pendleton seemed ageless. Of course, I'm certain that private trainers, a personal chef, and tons of cosmetic upgrades were at least partly responsible. But still, the guy had been born with enviable genetics. And his son . . . Well, let's just say that his son, who to this point in his life had lived off the grid as a bit of a recluse, was rumored to have followed in his father's footsteps when it came to charm and good looks.

My heart was pounding in my chest just like some sort of star-struck teenybopper about to meet her idol for the first time. Normally, I'm not overly impressed with megastars and their spoiled children, but Dirk Pendleton!

I'm certain my chin hit the pavement as an Adonis dressed only in a pair of swim trunks opened the front door. (Don't judge; you should see this guy.) He smiled at me, a look of delight on his gorgeous face, before complimenting me on my eyes, kissing me square on the mouth, and inviting us inside. Zak put his arm around my shoulders and pulled me close to his body. I'm not sure if it was to assert his ownership or simply to keep me from slithering to the ground as my legs turned to jelly. Either way, the gesture was appreciated. I realized at some point that I was supposed to walk forward, but my legs were too shaky to move. Zak, wonderful boyfriend that he is, took pity on me and diverted Dirk's attention as he took me by the arm and led me into the house.

"Your home is beautiful," I heard Zak say from what seemed like a million miles away.

"It's a house." Dirk shrugged. "I was out by the pool when you arrived. It's a beautiful day. Would you care to join me?"

"Huh." I tried to speak.

"We'd love to," Zak replied.

Zak led me to the patio while I tried to gather my senses. I knew I was being ridiculous. Dirk Pendleton Junior was just a man, and I already had the best man on the planet for a boyfriend. I really needed to get a grip. Zak scooted his chair close to mine as we sat down. I looked at his amused smile and grinned. He really was the best boyfriend.

"So you wanted to ask me some questions," Dirk said after pouring us each a large glass of whiskey without even asking if we wanted some. I don't particularly like whiskey, but I drank it anyway. Maybe the burn would jolt some sense into what had to be dormant teenage hormones.

"Yes," Zak answered. "We really appreciate your taking the time to help us with our project."

"You want to know about old Blakely's murder."

Even Zak looked surprised. "You figured that out, did you?"

"I had you checked out before you arrived. I check out everyone who comes onto my property. Do you have any idea how many lamebrain stories I get from paparazzi who want to snap a hundred-thousand-dollar photo of Dirk Pendleton's elusive offspring?"

"I guess I should have anticipated that," Zak conceded.

"Let me save you some time," Dirk began. "I didn't kill Porter Blakely, nor do I know who did. I don't have an alibi that I care to share for the time of the murder, but since I'm not in any way involved in his death, I'm not overly concerned about that. I might not have killed him, but I *was* blackmailing him."

"Come again?" I asked.

"Well, I'm not sure blackmail is the right word. Blakely's daughter, Megan, asked for my help in getting payback from her dad, and I agreed to do it. The whole thing was really just a big joke, so I'm not sure there will be any legal ramifications, but as a form of payback, it's priceless."

"Payback?" Zak asked.

"Blakely was an abusive man. According to Megan, who I have no reason not to believe, her father was so emotionally abusive to her mother that the poor woman killed herself when Megan was a young girl. Megan just recently turned twenty-one and received the money her mother left her. I guess she'd spent the past nine years planning a way to humiliate her dad for the way he'd humiliated her mother."

"Jack Frost," I realized.

"Very good." Adonis smiled at me. I had to blush and grin back. It would have been rude not to.

"Megan came to Ashton Falls shortly after she received the money. She knew what she wanted to do, but she needed leverage against her father, so she began snooping around in his private files when he wasn't at home. She stumbled across some records that indicated that Blakely had been instrumental in setting up intentionally bad investments that made him almost as much money as it lost his clients. She used the information to convince Blakely that it was in his best interests to jump through any hoops she might present. We came up with the idea for Jack Frost, the coldest man in literature. I got the costume and we put the plan in motion. It was hilarious."

Suddenly I felt just a tad annoyed with Dirk and his game. "It could have totally ruined our play."

"I'm sorry about that. I assure you that our intention was simply to humiliate Blakely. It's a shame he died. Megan had so many other creative ideas in store for the man."

"I've seen Blakely wearing the costume and enacting his part as Jack Frost. He didn't seem humiliated at all," I pointed out. "In fact, he seemed to really be into it."

"Yes, it was unfortunate that he took to the whole thing the way he did. Megan was disappointed that his horror at the idea seemed to turn to enjoyment after a short amount of time. I guess the man was a lot more twisted than we gave him credit for."

"You said Megan had other plans for humiliating her father?" I verified.

"She did, but the guy went and died on her. We talked about leaking photos to the press, in spite of the fact that the guy was no longer around to suffer the consequences of his humiliation, but Megan decided she'd lost interest in the game and left town a few days ago. She wants nothing to do with Ashton Falls, the bank, or the property. She's going to work out the details so that Washington gets the property he needs and then sell the place. I doubt she'll be back."

"And the bank?" I wondered.

Dirk shrugged. "There are other shareholders. I'm sure the attorneys will work it all out."

"Do you happen to know the names of the customers Blakely scammed?" I asked.

"Not off hand. Megan may have kept a list. I guess it wouldn't hurt to give you her e-mail address." Zak handed him a pen and a business card, which he scribbled on. "Be forewarned, though, that she's very bad about getting back to people. She's been on her own for a long time and isn't in tune with taking the needs of others into consideration."

"You met Megan recently?" I asked.

"We met a long time ago, when we were kids. Our fathers owned these adjoining properties, and we both had reason to want to keep low profiles, so we hung out a bit."

"Mr. Washington indicated that he'd never met Megan."

"Washington didn't build his house until six years ago, so he might not have met her. Megan used to spend summers here as a kid, but once she was old enough to have input into her own decisions, she stopped coming. I suppose her last visit prior to this one must have been when she was around twelve or thirteen."

I felt bad for Megan. Sure, I wasn't thrilled that her little trick on her dad almost ruined our play, but to grow up with such a cold and uncaring man for a father and to have your mother kill herself as a result of his abuse must have been unbearable. I wondered who raised her after her mother died but figured it wasn't relevant to the conversation so didn't ask.

"Okay, thank you for your time, and thank you for Megan's contact information," Zak concluded the conversation.

"No problem. It was lovely to meet you both. And maybe we can keep the Jack Frost thing between us?"

"Sure, no problem," I answered.

"So what now?" Zak asked we walked hand in hand back toward his truck. "It seems like we have some random pieces of a larger puzzle. Any suggestions about what to do to try to pull this whole thing together?"

"Dirk suggested that Blakely bilked some of his clients out of a lot of money. I'd be interested to know who exactly lost money due to his investment advice. I'd also be interested to know who might have a home or business in foreclosure with the bank."

"You know, it's possible Blakely's death had nothing to do with money," Zak pointed out.

"Maybe, but tracking down everyone who has a financial grudge against Blakely is a good place to start."

"That could be a lot of names. Most people in the area have or have had business dealings of one type or another with the man."

"I say we limit the search to people who have been hurt by him in the past six months. I don't suppose you can find your way into the banks records?"

"Not easily, but I know someone who can."

"Who?"

"Alice Jackson. She works in the accounting department of the bank. I'm sure she has access to most of the loan and deposit records."

"You know Alice?"

"I do some of my banking with the community bank, and as the institution's largest depositor, Alice and I are well acquainted."

I don't know why it never occurred to me that Zak might have money in the bank. He was exactly the type of guy to support local businesses, even if he did have plenty of money to spread around to the world's largest and most secure institutions.

"Do you think she'll tell us what we want to know?"

"Maybe if I ask real nice."

"How nice?" Uh-oh, Zoe the Jealous is about to make an appearance.

"Not that nice." Zak kissed my nose. "I could be wrong, but it's my guess that Alice will be more than willing to talk. My impression is that she's a nice woman who just happens to work for a bottom-feeder. I'll go to talk to her tomorrow morning, while you're at the birthing class with your mom."

Chapter 7

Monday, April 14

I was sorry my dad had decided he wasn't going to be able to act as Mom's birthing coach but thrilled to have the opportunity to do so myself. We'd gotten a late start, though, and while Mom was due to deliver in less than two weeks, we still had several classes to complete. Anyssa had agreed to let us attend the Monday class as well as our regularly scheduled Wednesday one so we might be able to catch up and gain all the information we needed for a painless and stress-free birth. The Monday class was held in the morning, and the clientele for that session was quite a bit different from the evening one. For one thing, the women tended to be younger. A lot younger. I recognized several women I'd gone to high school with, including the little sister of one of my closest friends. I hugged her and congratulated her on her impending delivery, all the while wondering what sort of insanity would make a twenty-year-old honor student want to be a mother at such a young age.

"Do you know if Anyssa has ever had any children?" Mom whispered to me as I massaged her belly and encouraged her to breathe.

"I don't think so. Why do you ask?"

"It's just that she keeps talking about our bodies as temples and birth as a spiritual experience, but not once has she mentioned hemorrhoids, gas, or stretch marks."

I laughed. "I guess she does have an idealized approach to the whole thing, but I've heard good things from some of the women I know who have taken her class."

"She talks about breathing slowly as our bodies release our offspring, but I seemed to remember quite a bit of screaming as the doctor had to pry you from your comfy napping place."

"Mine was a difficult birth?"

"It was. The doctor joked about the fact that you were snug and cozy and didn't seem to want to come out into the cold, hard world."

"Maybe Harper won't have the separation issues I did," I teased.

"Here's hoping," Mom said as she turned onto her side as instructed.

"Did you take classes before I was born?"

"No. The home for rich unwed women my parents sent me to embraced a more traditional approach."

"Traditional?"

"Drugs. Lots and lots of beautiful drugs."

"Do you plan to use drugs with this birth?"

"I'm hoping not to, hence the class."

Mom stiffened.

"Are you okay?" I asked.

"Just a twinge."

"Have you been having a lot of twinges?"

"A few," Mom admitted.

"Maybe Harper will come early."

"She can't come early; we still have four more classes."

I giggled. "I don't think she cares about classes. Was I early?"

"Actually," Mom rolled to the other side, as instructed by the group leader, "you *were* early. Five days early, if I remember correctly."

"If Harper comes five days early, she'll be born before Easter. Maybe we should get her an Easter basket just in case."

"She'd only be a day or two old. She won't care about a basket," Mom pointed out.

"Maybe not, but it *will* be her first Easter. She really should have one."

Mom sat up as the class finished. "Harper is lucky to have a big sister who thinks about these things. We're going to make a good team: you and me, and your dad."

"I think so too." I hugged Mom. "How about we go and look at baskets now, before I take you home? Just in case."

"I'd like that." Mom squeezed my hand. "That is, if I can figure out a way to get up off the floor."

I stood up and helped Mom to her feet. "Is it hard for you to talk about my birth?" I asked.

Mom slipped into the sweatshirt she'd worn over her tank top. "Sometimes. It was a very confusing time in my life. I loved and missed your father, but my parents had me convinced we couldn't be happy. And as much as I'd convinced myself that I wasn't ready to be a parent, when I held you in my arms after you were born, I knew I loved you and you'd always be a part of me. I even considered changing my mind and keeping you."

"So why didn't you?"

Mom shrugged. "I would have been a terrible mother. I *was* a terrible mother," she reminded me. "I knew in my heart that your dad would do a better job than I ever could. Still, the day they came to take you from me was the hardest one of my life."

"Dad would have let you be part of my life," I pointed out.

"I know. But I was young, and not a strong woman. Being near you but not being able to be with you hurt too much, so I left. I'm pretty sure I've regretted my decision every day since then, but I figured I'd made my life and all I could do was make the best of what I'd made."

"You won't leave with Harper?" I voiced the concern that had been nagging at me since I first found out my flighty mother was in Ashton Falls.

Mom took both of my hands in hers and looked me directly in the eye. "I won't leave with Harper."

By the time we finished shopping it was getting late. I dropped Mom at the house she was now sharing with Dad and headed back to the Zoo to check on things. Jeremy was on the phone when I walked through the door, but he waved me over as I entered the building.

"No problem," I heard him say. "Zoe or I will be there in less than fifteen minutes."

"Be where in fifteen minutes?" I asked.

"There's been an accident on the highway. One of our mama bears was hit by a car. She didn't make it, but she left behind a cub in need of rescuing. The man who called said he climbed a tree and won't come down."

"Has Fish and Game been called?"

"The man said they're on their way, but he wanted one of us to be there after what happened to that cub last fall."

"I'm on my way."

There'd been a similar situation last fall, and the guy from Fish and Game had handled things badly, and the baby had ended up dying. Residents in the area had been outraged, as they should be, and had begun calling us directly. The problem with that was that before we're allowed to take custody of large wildlife, the animals must be transferred to us officially by the public agency. Most times the transfer is painless, but every now and then we get a Fish-and-Game employee who decides to make things difficult. Which was why I was relieved to see that the person waiting for me was someone I had worked with before, Colin Brady.

"I thought you were going to retire after the first of the year," I greeted him.

"I intended to, but I had a bit of a financial setback," Colin replied.

"Well, I for one am glad you're still around. Some of these new guys don't know what they're doing."

"I hear yah."

"He's a little one," I commented as a cub who couldn't weigh more than ten pounds peered down at me through the tree branches.

"Yeah, it's a shame what happened to his mama."

"It seems like those bear-crossing signs we installed two years ago haven't slowed folks down at all," I commented.

"Everyone seems to be in a hurry nowadays," Colin agreed. "Guy who hit the mama didn't even stop, despite the fact that the impact sent the car spinning into the adjoining lane. Luckily, a motorist coming from the other direction saw what happened and called it in."

"You gonna tranquilize him?" I asked as I looked up into the tree at the tiny little bear cub. It broke my heart that the little guy would have to begin his life in the pen at the Zoo rather than in the forest with his mom. Taking care of orphaned babies was a large part of what Jeremy and I did, but with each new arrival my heart ached just a tiny bit more.

"I kinda hate to tranquilize the little guy while he's still up in the tree, given his size. I'm afraid he'll fall and be injured in the process, but he's pretty skittish, so I don't know that we have an option," Colin said.

I looked at the body of the mama bear, which had been pulled to the side of the road. The thought of the beautiful animal suffering such a senseless death brought tears to my eyes, but I realized she could be there for her cub one last time. "Why don't we try luring him down?" I suggested.

"Luring him?"

"Here's my idea," I began.

Colin and I dragged mama's body to the base of the tree, then hid out of sight. When the cub climbed down to join his mother, Colin tossed a net over him. Once he was trapped, we worked him into a crate, and I took him back to the Zoo while Colin dealt with the mama.

My heart was heavy as I drove toward town, but I knew that the little guy would be safe with us, and have the best chance for a normal life when he got a bit older. Jeremy and I took our guardianship of the wildlife entrusted to our care very seriously. We'd undergone hours of training and had access to the most comprehensive support network in the industry. Our goal was to care for the wildlife in such a way that they could be reintroduced into the wild as soon as possible.

"He all settled in?" I asked Jeremy two hours later.

"Snug as a cub in a rug," Jeremy assured me. "I thought I'd hang out here a while, just to make sure he does okay with his new situation, but you can go on home."

"Thanks. I'm sure Charlie is wondering where I've gotten off to."

"I was surprised to see he wasn't with you when you came in."

"I couldn't take him to the birthing class, and then Mom and I did some shopping. I really only intended to stop by for a minute to check on things and then head home. Hopefully, Zak got my message and went by to let him out. See you in the morning?"

"Yeah, I'll be in early. We're supposed to take delivery of those coyote pups from the valley by eight o'clock."

"I'll try to come in early as well."

Zak called as I was heading home and informed me that he had gotten my message and had taken Charlie with him to pick up takeout for dinner. He estimated that he'd be back to my place shortly after I arrived, but he was aware of my unpleasant task that afternoon and offered to keep things warm if I wanted to shower and change. I hate to admit that I cried in the shower. Okay, I sobbed. I always cry when one of our beautiful bears are so needlessly slaughtered. You'd think I'd be used to it by now, but the truth of the matter is that the loss of our wildlife is something I'll probably never get used to, no matter how long I do this job.

"So how did your lunch with Alice go?" I asked as I joined Zak in the kitchen as he was pouring some wine.

"Fine." He pulled me into his arms and kissed me on the top of my head. "Are you okay?"

"I will be." Leave it to Zak to see through my attempt to control my fragile emotions. "So about the investment scam . . . ?"

"Alice was unable to give me a list of men and women who lost money due to Blakely's bad advice, but, surprisingly, Megan answered the e-mail I sent yesterday."

"Any names pop?" I wondered.

"I went through the list Megan sent and eliminated all but four; many of the investors were from out of the area."

"Just because some of the investors didn't live around here doesn't mean they didn't do it," I pointed out.

"True, but we have to start somewhere, and the four people who live in town seemed the best place to start."

"And the four that were left?"

"Carson Worthington, Nick Benson, Phyllis King, and Dirk Pendleton Junior."

"Dirk? Odd he didn't mention it."

"What's odd is that he knew he'd be on the list but gave us Megan's contact information anyway," Zak said.

"Carson Worthington is your friend, isn't he? The one who owns the house Dad and Mom are buying?"

"He is. I doubt he did it, since he really is an all-around nice guy, but I suppose in all fairness we should keep him on the list until we can eliminate him."

"And I doubt Nick or Phyllis did it," I pointed out. Nick is a retired doctor and Phyllis a retired teacher, and both are longtime residents of Aston Falls and members of the book club Pappy and I belong to.

"None of the four stands out as a real suspect," Zak agreed.

"So what now?"

"We should see if we can check out everyone's alibi just to be safe. I'll contact Carson and Dirk, if you want to talk to Nick and Phyllis."

"Maybe Doug Barton really did do it," I said.

"Maybe. He sure seems to be the suspect who makes the most sense."

"As long as we're checking alibis, we should probably have a chat with Frank Valdez and Ernie Young. Both of them had reason to want Blakely out of the way, and while neither seems like a killer to me, it wouldn't hurt to have conversations with them."

"Okay, so we'll track everyone down tomorrow and see where we stand," Zak agreed.

"Did you learn *anything* from Alice?" I asked. "You did, after all, take her to lunch and turn on the charm. It seems like she could have told you something worthwhile."

"She didn't spill any bank secrets intentionally, but when I brought up Doug and the reason for his dismissal, she got very uncomfortable."

"You think she knows why Blakely canned him?"

"I think she might, but she isn't saying."

"That's frustrating."

"Actually, that's commendable. I certainly wouldn't want anyone working for me who was likely to blab about my business affairs, even if I were dead."

"Yeah, I guess you're right. I don't suppose we can get in to talk to Doug?"

"Doubtful."

"I wonder if he spoke to anyone before he was arrested."

"His wife?"

"Who skipped town," I reminded him. "Although it's possible she discussed things with her best friend before she left."

"And you know this friend?"

"I do. Her name is Nora Long. She adopted a sheltie from me last summer. I suppose I could drop in and see how things are going tomorrow."

"I guess it couldn't hurt." Zak nodded. "You up for a movie?"

"Nothing sad."

"Maybe an action flick?"

"Something with Dirk Pendleton Senior," I suggested. "I think we have several choices in your film library, if you want to go to your house."

"Seems like someone is crushing on Dirk Pendleton," Zak teased.

"I'm not crushing on anyone," I defended myself. (Okay, I might have been crushing on Dirk Junior just a tiny bit.)

"Not anyone?"

"Okay, maybe I'm crushing on you. But only if you stop teasing me."

"Okay." Zak pulled me into his arms and kissed me, making me forget all about the movie. "No more teasing."

"Well, a little teasing might not be bad," I said before I deepened the kiss.

Chapter 8

Tuesday, April 15

After Jeremy and I got the coyote pups checked in and settled, I decided to follow up with Nora Long, who worked for a local realty company. I didn't know her well, but in a small town like Ashton Falls, everyone knows everyone else to a certain degree. I decided to just pop in rather than call ahead for an appointment. She was the best friend of Doug's wife, Cleo, and I wasn't certain she'd be amenable to answering my questions. Perhaps if I caught her off guard, she wouldn't have time to think of an excuse not to see me.

"Zoe," Nora said as I walked through the front door of the office. Luckily, she appeared to be alone. "I was wondering when you'd wander in."

So much for a surprise attack.

"I imagine you're here to grill me about Doug Barton." Nora was a meticulously groomed woman who I guessed to be around forty. She was a go-getter who was well respected in the community, known for her tenacity as well as her sharp mind.

"I'm not sure that *grill* is the right word, but yes," I admitted to the stylishly dressed woman, "I did hope to have a few minutes of your time."

"Have a seat." She motioned to a pair of chairs on the other side of her desk.

"How did you know I'd be by?" I asked.

"From what I gather, you've been talking to everyone even remotely related to Porter Blakely's murder. I figured you'd get around to me eventually.

I'd like to specify up front that, while I'm not against telling you what I know, I'll only give you information I believe will help with the investigation. I'm not here to slur Cleo or reveal secrets I don't believe she'd want me to share."

"Fair enough. I'm primarily interested in why Blakely fired Doug."

Nora leaned back in her chair and began tapping one of her perfectly manicured nails on the desk. I figured she was running through a script in her mind, trying to decide what to share and what to keep to herself. "Doug first started working for Blakely a few months before the twins were born," she began. "I remember how thrilled he was to get the job; the family had been struggling financially, and the realization that they were having two babies was creating quite a bit of stress for both Doug and Cleo. Things seemed okay at first. Doug appeared to be doing well in his job and he received several promotions coupled with large raises within the first year. The family was able to buy a home and upgrade their vehicles. Everything seemed perfect until Cleo began getting backlash in town regarding some of Doug's business activities."

"Backlash?"

"What it boils down to is that after Doug took the job, Blakely began grooming him to take on more responsibility. Doug was ambitious and drank up the praise and money. Before long, he was doing most, if not all, of Blakely's dirty work."

"Dirty work?"

"Evicting tenants, raising rents, calling in loans, serving foreclosure notices, that type of thing. Most things were probably based on legitimate business decisions, but it seemed that Doug took a certain amount of glee in doing his job. He made a fair number of enemies, and it got to the point where poor, sweet Cleo couldn't so much as go to the grocery store without running into someone Doug had unhappy business dealings with."

"I can see how that would be really hard. It would be like being married to Scrooge."

"Exactly. Cleo begged Doug to quit. She wanted to move to a new town where they wouldn't be known and start over fresh, but Doug was having none of it. He insisted that the only way to provide for his family in the manner they deserved was to jump through Blakely's hoops."

"So why did Blakely fire him?"

"Doug was dispatched to a house to evict a family. The man insisted he'd made all his payments in a timely manner and had canceled checks to prove it. The family had been customers of the bank for quite some time and had never fallen behind on their mortgage, so the situation seemed odd to Doug. So odd, in fact, that he took it upon himself to do a little investigation to see if a mistake had been made. He found that while the payments had indeed been received by the bank, they'd been routed to the wrong account. He went to the boss to try to rectify the situation, but Blakely told him that the house had already been foreclosed on and it was much too late to stop the transfer of property because he'd already sold it to another party. It turns out the investor he'd sold the family's home to needed the land to build a parking lot for a project. The developer paid Blakely a lot of money for what amounted to a run-down little house."

I frowned. "I don't get it. If the man had been making his payments and there had been a clerical error, wouldn't the bank owe the man the money he had paid in?"

"Blakely told Doug that he would order an audit and make certain the man was paid everything that was due to him."

"But it was too late to save the house," I realized.

"Exactly. The property had been sold and the house was demolished while the audit was being conducted. Blakely ended up offering the man full market value plus twenty percent for the house that had been wrongly foreclosed upon."

"I guess that seems fair."

"Not at all. Remember that a commercial project was riding on this man's shabby little house. Without the parking area, the development couldn't happen. The developer had tried to buy the house from the man, but he'd refused to sell. Blakely saw an opportunity when he realized he held the note on the house, and that it carried one of his due-on-demand clauses, which allowed him to foreclose quickly if even a single payment was missed. The homeowner got fair market value plus some, but Blakely made ten times as much when he sold the house."

"So how did this lead to Doug being fired?"

"Blakely fired him for snooping around in files he wasn't authorized to access. Doug threatened to leak the fact that the entire fiasco had been fraud rather than an unfortunate clerical error, and Blakely threatened to ruin him."

"Could he do that?"

Nora shrugged. "Perhaps. Blakely was a snake, but he was a shrewd businessman who spared no expense when it came to his legal counsel. I'm sure both Doug and the homeowner would have gotten a court settlement if they'd pursued legal action, but Blakely had the resources to outlast either of the men in a lawsuit."

"Do you mind telling me why Cleo left?"

"She wanted to be done with the whole thing and get on with their lives, but Doug wanted revenge. He refused to leave town until he got his revenge, so Cleo took the kids and left without him."

"It really does sound like Doug might have done this," I said.

"Yes," Nora agreed. "I think he did."

"Tell me again why you're investigating Blakely's murder," Jeremy asked later that afternoon, as we both stood at the front counter of the Zoo sorting the paperwork from the morning's adoptions.

"Honestly," I looked at him helplessly, "I have no idea. I'm not personally involved in any way, like I've been in the past. I really should just let it go."

"So why don't you?"

"Maybe I will," I stated with certainty. I hadn't felt committed to this particular investigation from the get-go. I wasn't sure why I continued to pursue it, other than to satisfy my natural curiosity. "I'm almost positive Doug is guilty of killing Blakely and he's already being held. The only other leads we have are lame. Tracking down alibis when I already know the person is innocent is a waste of time."

"Who do you have left on your list?"

"I'm supposed to talk to Nick Benson and Phyllis King, and Zak's going to have conversations with Carson Worthington and Dirk Pendleton."

"*The* Dirk Pendleton?"

"Dirk Pendleton Junior," I clarified.

"Why in the world would he kill Blakely?"

I explained that they were neighbors and that Blakely had bilked Dirk, along with a handful of other locals, out of a good amount of money. And I told him about the list Zak had gotten from Blakely's daughter and the suspects who remained.

"You're seriously going to ask Nick Benson and Phyllis King for their alibis?"

"No," I admitted. "I guess not."

"Although . . ." Jeremy began, and then stopped.

"Although what?"

"I probably shouldn't say."

"Probably shouldn't say what?"

"I went bowling last night with the single parents group, and some of the folks from the senior center were there, including Phyllis. We got to talking, and she asked about Gina and Morgan. I told her about the baby shower you threw for me and mentioned that I really needed to look for a bigger place, and she told me that she has a two-bedroom town house she keeps as an investment that's coming available for rent."

"So? What does that have to do with Blakely's murder?"

"Probably nothing, but Phyllis did mention that the previous renters left because she'd been planning to put the place on the market. And that she was beginning to reconsider, since she'd recently come into some money, making the sale unnecessary. She said she'd prefer to keep it if she could find a responsible tenant."

I frowned. "Which doesn't jive with her losing a bunch of money in one of Blakely's schemes."

"Exactly."

"Maybe I *should* have a chat with her."

"Please don't mention that I said anything," Jeremy said. "Her town house seems perfect for Morgan and me, and she's willing to let me rent it at a huge discount if I let her babysit sometimes."

I smiled. Phyllis really was a sweetheart. "Don't worry, I won't say anything about our conversation. Chances are Phyllis simply has other investments, and one of them paid off."

"Probably. Phyllis seems like a smart woman. She not only congratulated Ellie on her new enterprise when she saw her but gave her some really good insight on marketing and tracking customer preferences as well."

"I'm sure Ellie appreciated that. It seems like Ellie's Beach Hut is doing well, but I know she's concerned about what will happen after the novelty wears off."

"Are you kidding? With her location, the place will be packed all summer, though come winter, things might get tight. She made the interior really welcoming, but it's pretty small. She'll need to figure out a way to do some sort of takeout service if she wants to maintain a steady volume."

"Ellie knows the restaurant business; she'll figure things out," I stated with confidence.

"I'm sure she will. Speaking of Ellie, I've been meaning to ask how she's doing," Jeremy added.

"What do you mean? You just said you saw her last night."

"I did, but she took off in the middle of the game. She seemed upset about something. I know the two of you are best friends, so I figured . . ."

"I haven't talked to her today," I said.

"Maybe it was nothing."

"Yeah, maybe. Still, I think I might stop by the pier on my way home."

"You can go now if you want. I can finish this paperwork and lock up."

"Thanks." I hugged Jeremy. "I'll see you in the morning."

By the time I got to Ellie's place, the afternoon crowd was beginning to clear out. I helped her clear tables as the few remaining patrons finished the last of their meals. It was a beautiful day, with temperatures reaching into the midsixties, and every one of the late-afternoon customers were sitting on the deck outside. I really love spring in Ashton Falls. The snow is melting and the lake and rivers are full. Waterfalls seem to spout up in all sorts of wonderful locations as seasonal creeks are filled with the runoff from high atop the mountain. Perhaps my favorite part of spring, however, are the daffodils that peek from beneath the snow, bringing color to the landscape. For me, the bright yellow flowers pushing their way to the surface through the last of the winter snow serves as a reminder of the wonder of nature and the rebirth of a new day.

"Something smells good in here." I took an appreciative sniff as I entered the Beach Hut.

"Probably the buffalo chicken I made for the Crock-Pot sandwich special of the day."

"It looks like they were a hit," I commented, based on the number of takeout containers in the garbage.

"They were. I think today was one of my best days, second only to the green chili shredded pork I did last week, although part of the business I enjoyed today could be due to the weather. Most of the snow has melted, and the beach was packed all day. I'm thinking of adding a couple more staff. If today is any indication of things to come, I'm not sure Kelly and I can handle the spring and summer crowd on our own. I'll need to talk to Mom, but I hope to have a minimum of three people on shift each day we're open during the summer. I'll need one to man the indoor counter, one to man the outdoor BBQ, and someone to clear tables."

"Are you going to extend your hours now that it's staying light longer?" Currently, the Beach Hut was open from 11 a.m. to 5 p.m.

"I really should stay open until seven if I want to attract the dinner crowd, but I don't want to get into a situation where I have to staff two shifts. Right now, Kelly or I come in at around ten and get everything set up, and we're rarely out of here before six by the time we clean up, so we already have an eight-hour day."

"I guess you could do four tens," I suggested.

"Could work."

"How is Kelly doing on the days she's here by herself?" Kelly and Ellie both worked Friday through Sunday, while Ellie covered Monday and Tuesday, giving Kelly two days off before she covered Wednesday and Thursday, giving Ellie two days off that she rarely took.

"Fantastic. She's really great. I'm actually thinking about making her more of a partner, so she won't ever consider quitting. I don't know what I'd do without her." Ellie opened the refrigerator to put the leftovers away. She began to rearrange things to make more room and came out with a six-pack of my favorite microbrew. "We have an hour before we have to be at the community center for rehearsal. Want to have a beer and sit out on the deck and watch the sun set?"

"Love to."

The sun was just beginning its descent toward the crystal-clear lake. In another half hour, the sky would begin to darken and the geese that flocked the beaches in the evenings, looking for scraps left over from the picnickers who frequented the area during the warmest part of the day, would begin to arrive. There's something magical and serene about sunset on the lake. Although the sun dips behind the mountain rather than the horizon, as it would on the ocean, most nights the sky is painted in bright reds, oranges, and, at times, purples, as the light gives way to the darkness.

"So what's up?" I asked as we sat down at one of the picnic tables near the water.

"What makes you think anything is up?"

I looked at Ellie. I knew she knew that I could tell when something was wrong. I figured if I waited, she'd share whatever it was that had caused the bags under her eyes.

"Rob and I had a date last night," she began

I waited in silence while she worked out what she wanted to say.

"He took me to dinner at the Wharf before we were supposed to meet the gang for bowling."

The Wharf is an upscale restaurant where Zak and I often ate.

"He told me that he wanted to talk about our future."

"Sounds serious." I hoped the man hadn't jumped the gun and proposed after only a few months of dating.

"I'm not sure serious is exactly the right word for the conversation, but it did have long-term implications. Hannah has started calling me Mommy now that she's getting old enough to start working out what a mommy is."

I cringed but didn't say anything.

"Rob said he wasn't pushing and he wasn't proposing, but it seemed to him that it might be time to have a discussion about where I saw our relationship going. He said he was at a place in his life where he was looking for a mother for Hannah. Someone he could build a family with. He wants her to have siblings close to her own age, and he felt it was time to ask me if I saw our relationship heading in that direction."

"And . . . ?"

"I love Hannah. I can totally see myself being her mother. I have to admit I've fanaticized about teaching her to dance and shopping with her when she gets a little older. She's so sweet and has a way of igniting every maternal instinct I possess. I feel so grounded when we spend time together."

"Grounded?"

"I guess *grounded* is a bit of a hippie-dippie word." Ellie laughed. "It's like I feel complete when I'm with her. It's as if my purpose in life is to be a mother, and when I'm with Hannah, I'm fulfilling my purpose, so I feel . . . grounded." Ellie looked at me. "I can't think of a better word."

"Does that mean you've decided to take things to the next level with Rob?"

"I don't know. Maybe. I'd be lying if I didn't admit that white picket fences and minivans have been very much on my mind lately. I guess I got caught up in the moment, but I found myself telling Rob as much. He's a really good guy and I think he loves me. He's kind and considerate and always looking out for my needs. Once he realized we might very well be on the same page, he told me about a house he was thinking of buying, and his plans and dreams for the future. It sounded wonderful."

"Yet I'm sensing a *but*."

"But nothing. Rob and Hannah are perfect for me. I really felt I was taking a positive step toward our future by having this discussion with Rob until Levi showed up at the bowling alley with some of the teachers from the high school. One look at him and . . ."

"And you realized you couldn't marry Rob if you were in love with Levi," I guessed.

"Something like that. I told Rob I wasn't feeling well and left."

I took Ellie's hand in mine from across the table. "What are you going to do?"

Ellie looked at me with tears in her eyes. "I don't know. I love Hannah. I can't imagine how awful it would be to walk away from her. And Rob and I are good together. We have the same values and goals. We enjoy being with the same people and we really have fun together. I'm certain I'd be happy if I married him. On the other hand, Rob is a great guy who deserves to have someone who loves him as much as he loves her. I want to love him. I guess I probably even do love him on some level, but as much as I know my infatuation with Levi can never go anywhere, it's still his smile that makes my heart pound."

"Levi may care about you more than you think."

"I know he cares about me. He's one of my best friends and he's always looked out for me, but Levi has a type. He's always dated tall blondes with big hair, big chests, and small waists. I'm tall and thin with straight brown hair and fairly plain features. Short of some major reconstruction by a top-notch plastic surgeon and hairdresser, there's nothing I can do that will make him see me as a potential lover."

Ellie could very well have a point. Levi had been acting jealous ever since Ellie began dating Rob, but jealousy didn't necessarily equate to desire.

"And even if I could find a way to spark his interest," Ellie continued, "Levi and I want different things at this point in our lives. I want the home filled with children and he's looking for temporary and uncomplicated. If we got together, neither of us would be satisfied, and we'd end up destroying our friendship."

Ellie was correct about that as well. It seemed she'd thought about this quite a lot.

"So what are you going to do?" I asked as the sun disappeared behind the mountain.

"Honestly? I have no idea. I feel like I should let Rob go so he can find someone who has eyes only for him, but I can't quite make myself walk away from Hannah. I keep thinking that I'll learn to love Rob the way he deserves to be loved, and even if I don't, we can still have a happy and comfortable life together."

"Have you talked to Rob about his feelings for you?" I asked.

"What do you mean?"

"I mean are there sparks? Do you think he feels the sparks for you that you've admitted you don't feel for him?"

Ellie frowned. "I've never even considered that. We've never even . . ." Ellie blushed. "I mean, we've kissed and stuff, but Rob knows I'm pretty old-fashioned in that respect and hasn't pushed."

"Maybe he feels the same way you do. Maybe you really are on the same page. Perhaps his main objective in your relationship is finding a mother for Hannah in the same way your main objective is being a mother to Hannah."

"Do you think that's enough?" Ellie asked. "Do you think you can build a marriage based on nothing more than a friendship between a man and a woman who share similar goals and interests?"

"If you're looking for relationship advice, I'm afraid you're barking up the wrong tree," I reminded her. "My score card with men in general has been pretty dismal."

"Your relationship with Zak is far from dismal."

"Thanks to him. He seems to know what a relationship should look like, and he's been very patient, waiting for me to catch up."

"But there are sparks?" Ellie asked.

"Oh, yeah. There are sparks. But I don't think the sparks are the main thing we have between us. I think it's our friendship that I hold closest to my heart."

"Friendship is important. Sparks can fade, but friendship lasts forever," Ellie pointed out.

"Maybe, but the sparks can be nice while they last."

Ellie smiled.

"Do you think that Hannah is clouding the picture?" I asked.

"What do you mean?"

"Would we be sitting here discussing whether or not you should make a commitment to Rob if Hannah wasn't part of the deal?"

Ellie looked surprised. "No," she said, "we wouldn't." She sighed with what looked like relief at having come to a conclusion. "I need to talk to Rob."

"Yeah. I think you do."

Chapter 9

Wednesday, April 16

"Six dogs, three cats, all checked in." Jeremy handed me a pile of paperwork to review. The Bryton Lake shelter, once again filled to capacity, had sent the short-timers over that morning. "One of the dogs is pregnant. Very pregnant," Jeremy emphasized. "One of us should probably take her home until after she delivers, but I'm afraid my place is packed with all the baby shower gifts I have yet to find a place for. Besides, my apartment building doesn't allow dogs."

I remembered the heartbreak of losing Maggie, the last dog I'd fostered, and almost declined but then thought better of it. The dog, Sophie, clearly needed me. "I'll take her. Do we have an idea of when she's supposed to deliver?"

"According to Scott, any day now."

I frowned. "And the Bryton Lake shelter had her on the short-timers list?"

Jeremy shrugged. "Apparently. I guess she's been at the shelter for most of her pregnancy. According to the records, it looks like she was brought in by her family almost six weeks ago. Chances are the fact that she was pregnant kept interested parties from adopting her. She's a cute little thing."

I looked at Charlie, who was staring up at me with the sweetest face. "How about it? Are you up for some company?"

Charlie barked.

"Okay, I guess I should go and meet my newest houseguest." I sorted through the files that Jeremy handed me until I found the right one. Sophie was a terrier mix weighing close to forty pounds. She was two years old and had lived with the same family since she was a puppy. The dad had been transferred to another state for his job as an engineer and the family felt they couldn't commit to keeping the dog. It was only after they'd checked her into the shelter that they'd discovered she was pregnant.

I asked Jeremy to take Charlie into the front with him, set the file on my desk, and headed down the hall. I unlocked the pen, attached a leash to Sophie's collar, and led her back to my office. I closed the door, unhooked the leash, and knelt down on the floor. Sophie scurried beneath the desk.

I called to her gently as she peered out at me with the saddest eyes. "It's okay, sweetie. Let's take a look at you."

Sophie began to whine but didn't move from her protected location.

"It looks like you've had a hard time, but you'll like it at the boathouse. Charlie is really great and will make a good friend, and you'll have two cats to terrorize."

Sophie inched forward just a bit.

"And my boyfriend Zak is notorious for sneaking chunks of meat to the animals when he thinks I'm not looking," I continued in what I hoped was a soothing voice. "Although," I qualified, "I suppose we should follow the diet Scott left for you. I'm really glad your babies won't be born in doggie jail."

I wondered if Bryton Lake would have euthanized the expectant mom if we hadn't been open and able to take her. Probably. The thought made me want to cry.

"I still have a nice doggie bed left from my previous guest. I think you'll like it. If nothing else, it will be nicer than the hard cement floor you've been sleeping on."

Jeremy opened the door a crack. "Want some help?"

"She seems a little skittish."

"Not at all." Jeremy walked into the room, and Sophie waddled her way over to him. She sat at his feet while he leaned down to pet her.

"Wow, she really likes you. It's too bad you can't take her."

"I'd love to, but it's not practical right at the moment. I'm sure she'll love you once she gets to know you."

I had to admit I was feeling a bit wounded that Sophie so clearly preferred Jeremy to me. I mean, Jeremy is a nice guy with a gentle way about him, but animals of all kinds usually love me, and the fact that Sophie seemed to be afraid of me was like a knife to the heart.

"Have you spent much time with her?" I wondered.

"No, we just seemed to hit it off. Should I let Charlie in?"

I shrugged. "Might as well see how it goes."

Luckily, Sophie loved Charlie, and the feeling seemed to be mutual, so I didn't see a problem in bringing the little dog home. I'd planned to leave early anyway, so maybe I'd just let Sophie hang out with me in the office until I was ready to go. I was sure that once she got to know me, she'd get over her obvious fear of me.

"I can keep an eye on both dogs until you get back from your meeting with Salinger," Jeremy offered.

"What meeting with Salinger?" I asked.

"The two o'clock meeting I confirmed for you this morning."

I must have had a blank expression on my face because Jeremy added, "You were cleaning the bear cage and I poked my head in and told you that Salinger wanted to meet with you today. I asked if two o'clock would work and you sort of grunted. I took that as an assent and told Salinger you'd be by at the requested time."

I did remember something about a meeting, now that Jeremy mentioned it. I'd been distracted, thinking about the small argument I'd had with Zak last night concerning the frequency of his business meetings. We rarely argue, and the fact that he'd returned home rather than staying over and then left on his trip this morning without stopping by had me more than a little upset. I don't know why I turn into such a nag when Zak has to go away. He'd been a busy software developer who traveled a lot when I first got together with him, so I don't know why I should expect anything different now. I really owed him an apology. A big one. I'd call him before heading out to my meeting.

I looked at the clock. Or perhaps I'd call after my meeting; it was already a quarter till two. "I should head out. Call Scott and tell him I'm taking Sophie home. Ask him if there are any special instructions.

After that, get her vitamins and everything together. I'll plan to get her settled in as soon as I get back."

Luckily, Salinger was ready and waiting when I arrived, so I didn't have to spend the entire afternoon waiting around for him. His secretary led me to a viewing room and explained that the sheriff would be right with me. I groaned when I imagined waiting in the dark little room for hours on end, but Salinger came in just a few minutes later.

"Thank you for coming down," he began. "I'd like you to take a look at the lineup we've prepared and tell me if you recognize the man you saw leaving the bank on the night Blakely was killed."

"I told you, the man had on a costume. I didn't see anything."

"Just humor me," Salinger said. "Send them in," he instructed whoever was on the other side of the two-way radio he held.

In walked five people, all dressed as the Easter Bunny. "Do any of these outfits look familiar?"

"Where did you find so many bunny costumes?" I was awed.

"Four are from rental shops; the other is privately owned. Try to imagine this is the night you found Blakely dead. Do any of these costumes look like the one you saw?"

I tried to remember what I'd seen. It had been dark and snowy, and the bunny was running away from me. Salinger told the bunnies to turn around. The lights were dimmed, and he asked me to concentrate on exactly what I'd seen. I began to sweat. I suspected that one of the bunnies was a new suspect and knew if I guessed right but wasn't certain, I could get an innocent man arrested.

"It definitely wasn't number three or five," I decided.

"Why do you say that?"

"The ears on number three stick up, and my bunny had droopy ears. Also, my bunny was a dark color—brown, I think—and number five is white."

"Okay, excuse numbers three and five," Salinger spoke into his radio. "And the others?"

I continued to study the remaining three rabbits. All were a brownish color with droopy ears. Two of the rabbits were tall—over six feet with the head—and the third rabbit was quite a bit shorter. "I don't think it's number two. My bunny was taller, I think, although," I qualified, "it was dark and snowing. I really can't be a hundred percent sure."

"Why do you think the bunny was tall if you couldn't see that well? Perception in a snowstorm can be tricky."

I thought about that. I'd been sure the bunny was tall. Why had I gotten that idea in the first place? Salinger was right; things look different in the dark. I remember watching the bunny run away and wondering if I was seeing things. I remember turning to head into the bank just as . . . "The tree," I said. "The bunny had to duck to get under the branch of the tree in the field behind the bank. I've walked under it with no problem many times, so the bunny must have been taller than I am. I'd estimate that he'd need to be at least six feet tall to have to duck. You can measure the branch, if you'd like."

"We will, but I agree with you. The branch is about six feet off the ground. Release number two," Salinger instructed. He turned to look at me. "Can you narrow it down further?"

I looked at the two remaining bunnies. Both were the same color and about the same height. The fine detail that made each costume distinct couldn't really help me; I'd only seen the back and it had been dark. I tried to think of anything that might distinguish one from the other, but I was coming up blank.

"I'm sorry," I said, "but I don't think I can narrow it down any further. Is the suspect one of the two remaining rabbits?"

"He is," Salinger confirmed.

"And it isn't Doug Barton?"

"It is not."

"So Doug is most likely innocent," I concluded.

"Perhaps, although bringing a second suspect into the mix doesn't necessarily mean that the first one is innocent. I'll need to do a bit more digging before I can be certain."

"I don't suppose you can tell me the identity of the two remaining bunnies?"

Salinger paused. "I'm sorry, but until an arrest is made, I can't."

"I understand."

"That should do it for now." Salinger stood up and opened the door. "I'd appreciate it if you kept this to yourself until after the arrest has been made and a statement has been issued."

"Yeah, okay." I stood up and walked through the door.

"And Zoe" Salinger stopped me. "If you think of anything else, you'll let me know?"

"Yeah, I'll let you know."

"Thank you. I'd appreciate that."

I went through everything in my mind as I drove back to the Zoo. It didn't take me long to figure out where I'd seen the bunny costume in the lineup before.

"So?" Jeremy asked when I walked in. Charlie ran up to greet me and Sophie followed along as if she'd actually missed me. I knew she was simply aping Charlie, but I'd take what I could get.

"Salinger wanted me to participate in a lineup. He hoped I could identify the man I saw running away from the bank."

"I thought you saw a rabbit."

"I did. All five men were wearing rabbit costumes."

"Really? Sorry I missed that. Did you pick out the guy?"

"I narrowed it down to two, but Salinger is pretty convinced he's got his man."

"No kidding. Who did it?"

I hesitated. "Salinger wouldn't say who his suspect was, but I think I figured it out."

"Who is it?" Jeremy asked again.

"Who in town has an Easter Bunny costume?" I asked.

"Not your grandpa!" Jeremy was clearly shocked.

"No, not Pappy. Think harder."

Jeremy screwed up his face as he pondered the question. I could almost see a lightbulb come on the moment he realized the answer. "Frank Valdez."

"Bingo."

"Frank? Really? He doesn't seem like the type to kill a man."

"I agree."

"Do you think Salinger will arrest him?"

"My gut tells me no, unless he has additional proof that I'm not privy to. As far as I can tell, all he really has to go on is the fact that Frank owns a bunny suit and is about the same height as the man I saw running from the bank."

"Wow, who would have thought?"

"I think I'll pop by his store on the way home to see if he's there. Maybe if I ask him what's going on, he'll tell me. Oh, drat."

"Oh drat what?" Jeremy asked.

"I forgot that I promised Gilda I'd come to the rehearsal. I hate to leave Sophie alone her first night in the boathouse, and I have Lambda as well. Do you think you could hang out at the boathouse for a couple of hours and keep an eye on the dogs? I have some new movies you can watch, and plenty of food you can help yourself to."

"Can I bring Jessica and Rosalie?"

"Jessica and Rosalie from the adoption clinic?"

"Yeah. I took your advice and introduced myself, and we've been hanging out. We were going to watch a movie tonight, but I'm sure they'd just as soon watch it at your place."

"Certainly you can bring them. And thank you so much for doing this. I shouldn't be all that long."

"Take your time. Your boathouse is much more comfortable then the saggy sofa in my apartment."

"Is Jeremy dating this woman?" Ellie asked me while we waited for the kids to change into their costumes.

"I don't think they're dating. She's exactly his type, but she has to be a few years older than he is, and he *is* expecting a baby any day by another woman. Jessica and Rosalie are new in town, so I'm pretty sure Jeremy is just being neighborly."

"He should bring them to the single parents mixer tomorrow night."

"I'll mention it to him when I get back to the boathouse."

"It's just pizza and a Disney movie at the house of one of the single moms, but it would be a good time for Jessica to meet the parents and Rosalie to meet the kids."

"How many single parents are in the group?"

"It varies. There are usually ten families or so at each event, but the members who attend aren't always the same. If I had to guess, I'd say we have twenty or so single parents who participate on a semiregular basis."

"Are we ready?" Gilda asked through a microphone.

"Ready over here," Ellie replied.

"Okay, we're going to take it from the top. Zoe, I need you to be sure that the eggs stay behind the yellow line and that none of them trip over the others."

"Got it," I responded.

"And Easter Bunny—"

"Yeah?" Pappy, dressed in full costume, poked his head through the closed curtain.

"Your cue to come in is the first word of the second verse of the song."

"Okay, I got it."

"Okay, start the music."

The next two hours were hysterical as we tried to get the kids to act more adultlike and the adults to act more childlike. The play wasn't going to win any awards based on the script, acting, lighting, or sound, but it was fun and entertaining, and the kids were adorable. While I needed an aspirin with a vodka chaser by the time the rehearsal was over, Ellie looked like she was in her element. She really was going to be a great mom one day.

"Wasn't it fantastic?" Ellie came jogging up with her face flushed and her hair messy.

"It was something, all right," I agreed.

"Those kids are all so cute. Every time I think I have a favorite egg, one of the others does something adorable."

"The play is going to be great."

"I guess we should help Gilda and Hazel clean up."

"Yeah, I guess we should. Do you want to come over after?" I asked. "Zak is out of town, and I want you to meet Sophie. Besides, you can also meet Jessica and Rosalie. It will be nice for Jessica to have a female friend in the single parents group."

"Yeah, I'd like that. Give me twenty minutes."

As predicted, Jessica and Ellie hit it off, and both Jessica and Rosalie seemed excited about attending the single parents group the following evening. After Jeremy and the others left, Ellie and I poured glasses of wine. It had been a long day and I was exhausted, but it was nice to spend some quiet time with my best friend.

"I heard Levi asked Carly Wilder out," Ellie commented after we'd settled onto the sofa.

"Yeah, he mentioned that he might."

"They don't really seem to be a good fit to me."

"I have to agree, although Levi is just looking for someone to spend time with. It's not like he's in the market for a serious relationship, so it could work out okay. Did you ever talk to Rob?"

"Actually, we had lunch together."

"And?"

"I'm not sure how he did it, because I was certain I'd made up my mind after our talk yesterday, but Rob managed to convince me to continue with the relationship. He acknowledged that it might not be built on a strong physical attraction, but we have a lot going for us, and he thinks we have a solid foundation for the future."

"And you agree?"

Ellie looked at me. "For now I do. If you compare my relationship with Rob and my relationship with Levi, it's clear I feel more of an attraction toward Levi, and he *is* one of my best friends. I love him and would trust him with my life, but I'm not sure I trust him with my happiness. He tends to have a wandering eye and has commented on many occasions that he isn't ready to have children. In fact, he's said more than once that he's not sure he *ever* wants children."

"True," I acknowledged.

"Rob, on the other hand, is also a good friend with whom I share common goals, and while he might not get my engine running the way Levi does, his kisses are pleasant. I have to ask myself, who, in the long run, will make me happier? Someone who makes my palms sweat or someone who shares my dream for the future?"

"I hear what you're saying, but you're only twenty-four. Maybe the person you'll end up with doesn't have to be an either/or choice. Maybe there's someone out there who'll provide the opportunity for a great big *and.*"

"I guess that's why I hesitate to become overly serious with Rob, but I also don't think I'm ready to walk away. Maybe I just need more time to think about it."

"And Hannah?"

"Yeah, she's an issue, but Rob assured me that even if we decide to stop dating, I can continue to spend time with Hannah and will always have an honorary position as Aunt Ellie."

"Sure, until he finds a new girlfriend who isn't fond of having the old one around."

"You think that could happen?"

"I'd be amazed if it didn't. I love you and want you to be happy," I assured Ellie. "All I ask is that you take some time to really think things through. Making a decision to walk away will be difficult now, but if you continue with the relationship and it doesn't work out, it will be twice as hard to leave a year or two from now."

"Yeah, okay. I see your point."

"Great. So how about a Dirk Pendleton movie? Zak brought one over, but we never got around to watching it."

"I still can't believe you met the son. Was he as gorgeous as his photos?"

I shrugged. "He was okay."

Chapter 10

Thursday, April 17

The next morning, I called Jeremy and told him I planned to drop in on Frank on my way to work. My mom agreed to come over and sit with the dogs, and my dad promised to look in on everyone once Pappy arrived at Donovan's to relieve him.

I hoped I could catch Frank at his store before it opened. I knew that he normally parked in the back alley, so I drove around to the back and looked for his car. Luckily, it was right where I hoped it would be. I rang the bell and waited for Frank to answer.

"Zoe," Frank greeted me. "I was hoping you were the guy with my canoes."

Frank owns Outback Hunting and Fishing, a rugged, outdoorsman's type of place that's decorated in tones of brown and green and features a variety of animal heads hanging from every wall. I have to confess, the store isn't my favorite place to visit, but Frank is a nice guy, despite his propensity for killing the very animals I work to save, and I wanted to help him out if I was able to do so.

"Sorry, no canoes. I would like to talk to you, though, if you have a minute."

Frank hesitated. I was pretty sure he knew why I was there, but I stood there smiling innocently. "Yeah, okay, come on in."

Frank led me through the store to his office. "What can I help you with?"

"You were the bunny I saw running from the bank on the night Blakely was killed."

"I'd hoped you didn't see me. Did you tell Salinger? Is that why he called me in for that lineup?"

"Actually, it didn't occur to me that the bunny was you until I saw the lineup. I guess in this case Salinger was one step ahead of me. Do you want to tell me what happened?"

"Just because I own a bunny costume doesn't mean I killed Blakely," Frank pointed out.

"True. But that was you running from the bank, and we both knew I would figure out what was going on eventually. I know you, Frank, and I'm having a hard time believing you'd kill anyone, but Salinger is pretty sure you're guilty, and once he gets the proof he needs, you'll be arrested for Blakely's murder. If you didn't do it, let me help you."

Frank stood up and began to pace around the room. I knew he was considering my offer, and I decided to let him work it out on his own. I'd been certain Frank was the rabbit I saw ever since the lineup, but I still had a hard time believing he killed Blakely, despite the rumors of his eminent foreclosure.

"I didn't kill Blakely," Frank began, "but I am guilty of a crime, or at least a potential crime. I was there to rob the bank."

"What?"

"It's not as bad as it sounds," Frank assured me. "Well, maybe it is, but please believe me, I had no idea anyone would end up dead."

"Perhaps you should start at the beginning," I suggested.

"After Michael's legal trouble last fall, I had to take out a loan on my house to pay the attorney fees. I'd already borrowed quite a bit to remodel the store, so I couldn't qualify for any type of conventional loan. Blakely said he'd agree to a hard money loan because I was one of his better customers. I can't tell you how relieved and grateful I was. I guess I was so desperate to get the money that I didn't look things over as carefully as I should have. What I didn't know at the time was that I'd signed a contract with an on-demand clause, which basically states that if I'm late on even one payment, Blakely has the right to demand payment in full. And if payment isn't received immediately, he has the right to take my home, which I freely offered as collateral. We had a slow winter at the store, and I missed a couple of payments. I received a notice of foreclosure about six weeks ago. There's no way I could come up with the balance of the loan, and Blakely knew it."

I waited while Frank gathered his thoughts. It sounded like he had the same type of loan the man Nora told me about did. Blakely really was a snake to take advantage of people the way that he had.

"A few weeks ago, Doug Barton came into the store to buy some ammo," Frank continued. "I knew he used to work at the bank and we got to talking. He told me that I wasn't the first person Blakely had pulled this on. He said the reason he was fired was because he challenged Blakely on his decision to foreclose on another family who were longtime customers of the bank and didn't deserve what they got. And that there was a group of people who'd decided to exact their own revenge since Blakely seemed to have enough money and legal resources to outlast a legitimate lawsuit. Barton said he knew where Blakely's private safe was located and was certain he could disable the cameras and alarms so that his team could get into the bank after-hours. Our plan was to steal the contents of Blakely's private safe, which Doug assured me contained not only money and other valuables but proof of Blakely's dirty business practices. Fool that I am, I agreed to help."

"Why the bunny costume?"

"Doug said we'd need to access the security room to get to the safe, and the cameras in that room were set up with fail-safes that couldn't be disabled. Everyone in the group was to wear a costume that concealed his identity. I guess I should have thought through my choice a little better and rented something, but I didn't want there to be a paper trail back to the outfit I wore, and I had the bunny costume hanging in my closet."

"So what happened?"

"I had car trouble and got to the bank late. The door was cracked open, so I went in and found Blakely's body."

"Everyone else had left?"

"It appeared so."

"Okay, so other than Doug, who else was involved?"

"I have no idea. The idea of the costumes wasn't only to conceal our identities from the cameras but from each other as well. I think there were five of us in total, but Doug is the only one I had any contact with."

"You need to tell Salinger what you know."

"He'll arrest me for my intention to rob the bank."

"Would you rather he arrest you for murder?"

"No." Frank sighed. "I guess not."

"Come on. I'll go with you and we can talk to him together."

"I should call someone to open the store."

"I can wait."

Although Thursday is book club night and I normally try to attend, I'd ended up being out all day and didn't want to leave the dogs home alone. I usually take Charlie with me to the event, but I didn't think Sophie was up to making the trip into town. If I had to bet, I'd say she was going to deliver within the next few days. I called Pappy to explain why I wouldn't be there, and he informed me that they were only having a small group that night, and suggested that they come to me. I readily agreed to host the meeting and spent the next hour making my boysenberry cookie bars for dessert.

When I'd first joined the book club, twenty seniors attended on a regular basis. Several had moved away, a few others had died, and a handful had found that they were no longer able to get around in the evenings. As of late, the number of attendees hovered around six, myself included. Perhaps it was time to recruit some new members.

Pappy was the first to arrive, followed by Hazel Hampton, who came with Phyllis King. I watched as Hazel sat down next to Pappy, who seemed to light up when she joined him. Perhaps the rumor that the two were sweet on each other was more than a rumor after all. Phyllis took charge of making sure that everyone had coffee and dessert as they filed in. Nick Benson arrived after Hazel and Phyllis, with Lilly Evans bringing up the rear.

"Are we all here?" I asked.

"'Fraid so," Hazel said. "Before we begin our discussion of the book, I think we should decide whether or not we want to try to recruit new members. Personally, I'm conflicted. On one hand, having a larger number creates a more diverse conversation, but on the other, if we keep it small, maybe we can begin meeting at members' homes. I have to say that meeting here is much nicer than meeting at the library, and if we take turns being host, it shouldn't be too much of a burden on any one person."

"I like the small group," Nick joined in, "although I wouldn't mind evening out the number of men and women a bit. Ever since Tanner died and Larry moved, the vote has been skewed toward books of a romantic nature. Not that I mind an occasional romance, but a good thriller would be a nice change."

"I usually don't vote," I pointed out. "If we want to keep it small, the addition of one male would even things out to three and three."

"I think Ethan Carlton might be interested," Phyllis suggested. Phyllis was a retired English teacher and Ethan was a retired history professor.

"Why don't you ask him, and we'll table the discussion to next meeting?" Hazel suggested. "So about the book . . ."

"I heard they arrested Frank Valdez," Nick said.

"Frank?" Phyllis gasped. "Whyever would they arrest Frank?"

"I heard he tried to rob the bank."

"What?" almost everyone in the room replied.

Nick filled the group in on what he'd heard, while I bit my tongue and tried not to interrupt. I'd promised Salinger I wouldn't share the outcome of our meeting, but it appeared that the Ashton Falls gossip hotline had managed to find out most of what was going on without my help. Nick had most of it right. As the group speculated on why Frank might sink to such an act and who he might have been working with, I reviewed in my mind my own list of suspects.

Frank had told Salinger that Doug had approached him, and that there were at least three others, though at no time had Doug revealed their identities. He did indicate that the team, who referred to themselves as the cartoon bandits, was made up of people who had been scammed out of their money or property by Blakely. Based on the little bits of information Zak had managed to obtain, the list was a long one that included both Nick and Phyllis. I watched both closely as the group debated whether Frank was a hero or a fool. Neither admitted to being Blakely's victims, but neither appeared overly secretive either. I doubted that either was part of the comical group of thieves, but until I'd spoken to Frank, I wouldn't have thought him capable of taking part in such a misguided scheme either.

"Salinger is holding Doug and Frank. Both have admitted to their parts in the robbery scheme, but neither has admitted to being responsible for Blakely's death," Nick revealed.

"Frank said he arrived after Blakely was dead and the others had left, but Doug was supposed to arrive first and was responsible for disabling the camera and alarm, so he must know the identity of the others," I blurted out before I realized I'd just jumped into a conversation I had no business being a part of.

"I wondered when you'd tell us what you know." Pappy chuckled.

"Yes, do tell us," Hazel encouraged.

I spent the next ten minutes filling the others in on my conversation with Frank at the store, and then with Frank and Salinger at the sheriff's office. (Note to those reading this: never tell me a secret you don't want revealed. I obviously am terrible at keeping my mouth shut even when I have every intention of doing so.)

"Doug told Salinger that he only knew the identity of one other member, the man who recruited him."

"And who was that?" Phyllis was sitting on the edge of her seat.

"A man by the name of Arthur Berry. He seems to be the man who was the catalyst for Doug being fired. Supposedly, Arthur came to him a few weeks ago, saying he'd been recruited by someone else whose name he wasn't at liberty to reveal. It seems the sting was set up so that person one recruited person two, and person two was told to recruit a third person without revealing the identity of person one. That way each member of the team only knew the identity of the person who recruited him and the person he recruited, and no one had the full roster."

"That was smart of person one," Pappy commented. "In this scenario we should assume that person two is someone person one trusted to keep his mouth shut."

"It *was* a good plan. Each member of the team was supposed to show up at the appointed day and time wearing a costume that wouldn't reveal his identity. Doug said he got there first and hid in a cleaning closet. He changed into his Batman costume, complete with an enclosed hood, which he'd left there on a previous visit. After the bank closed, he snuck out of his hiding place and disarmed the alarm and all the cameras, except the ones in the security room, which can't be tampered with. Then he went to the back door and let in Santa Claus, Darth Vader, and someone dressed as one of the gorillas from the movie *Space Apes*. The fifth member, who turned out to be Frank, hadn't yet arrived. Doug said he left the door cracked open."

"Did he know who the others were?" Phyllis asked.

"No. He said he was pretty sure Santa was Arthur Berry, the man who'd recruited him, but the other two also had costumes with enclosed heads, so he had no idea who they were. Doug believed Frank was the end of the line, so the gorilla and Darth Vader must have been recruits one and two. Most likely those were the men who came up with the idea in the first place."

"Why did they continue with the plan when they realized Blakely hadn't left?" Pappy asked.

"Doug insisted that they didn't know he was still on the premises. He thinks Blakely must have been in the bathroom during the time the men came in and made their way down the hall. At some point Blakely must have heard them, because he showed up during the operation. Doug said that when they first heard Blakely coming, they hid. Blakely saw that the door to the security room was open and went inside. The gorilla went to the door of the security room, Blakely saw him and started toward him, and the gorilla shot him. At that point they all ran."

"This is like the plot of a really bad movie," Pappy commented.

"I hear you," I agreed.

"I get why this Arthur recruited Doug, because he could get into the bank and disarm the alarm, but why did Doug recruit Frank?" Nick asked.

"According to Doug, Frank provided the guns, as well as some surveillance equipment."

"So all Salinger needs to do is work backward," Pappy realized. "If Doug was recruited by this Arthur, then Arthur will know who recruited him, and that person will know the identity of man number one."

"That's the plan," I confirmed, "but as of this afternoon, Arthur was nowhere to be found."

"I suppose it wouldn't hurt to contact costume rental shops in the area to see who rented a Darth Vader or gorilla costume," Hazel suggested.

"Perhaps, but Doug said those costumes looked really professional. Like movie costumes."

Movie costumes. Suddenly I knew exactly who I needed to talk to.

Chapter 11

Friday, April 18

Unfortunately, Dirk, like Arthur, seemed to have flown the coop. I went by his house, but his housekeeper told me that he was out of town and wouldn't be back until late that evening at the earliest. I thought about mentioning the costume angle to Salinger but decided to wait until I'd had a chance to speak to Dirk. If Salinger questioned Dirk, it would find a way into the news even if Dirk was innocent. I wanted to have a chat with the man, get a feel for his degree of guilt or innocence, and then figure out my next move. I knew how much Dirk valued his privacy and didn't want to be responsible for a media storm if it turned out that he wasn't involved in the scheme, as I thought.

After stopping off at Dirk's, I headed to the Zoo. Mom had agreed to sit with Sophie again, and I really needed to get caught up on some paperwork. Since Sophie seemed to love Mom and was also comfortable with Dad's dogs, I decided to take Sophie to Mom's place and bring Charlie and Lambda with me to the shelter. Mom suggested that I stay for dinner when I came by to pick up Sophie, and I agreed.

I was pretty sure Mom was interested in adopting Sophie after she gave birth. Maybe it was the shared pregnancy discomfort, but Mom seemed quite taken with the little dog. Dad already had two dogs, but the house they shared was large and would easily accommodate Sophie, should Mom decide to keep her. I considered suggesting that Mom just take her now, but given the fact that she was about to deliver her own little bundle of joy, I didn't want her to have to deal with puppies.

"Thank God you're here," Jeremy greeted me at the door the moment I arrived. "I just got a call from Gina. She's at the hospital."

"You're going to be a dad." I smiled.

"Yeah, I really am." Jeremy grinned back "But I really have to go. We have three adoptive parents picking up pets today. The files are on the counter. And someone from the Forest Service is coming by to check on the cub from the car accident."

"Go, just go," I encouraged. "I can handle this."

"Thanks." Jeremy hugged me one final time and was out the door.

Later that afternoon, I was beginning the final feeding of the day, as well as the final exercise session for the dogs, when the phone rang. "Hey, Jeremy. Is Morgan here?"

"No, she isn't. It's a disaster. It looks like Gina is going to have to have a C-section and I'm totally freaking out."

"C-sections are quite common," I said, trying to comfort the nervous father-to-be.

"But I didn't plan for a C-section. I planned for a quick and easy natural birth."

"There's nothing quick and easy about first babies."

"Now you tell me. What am I going to do?"

"I don't think you have to do anything. I've never had a baby, but I'm pretty sure the doctor and mom take care of everything."

"You don't understand." I could hear Jeremy pacing as he spoke. "A C-section is an operation. It requires a hospital stay. I can't afford a hospital stay. I could barely afford a natural delivery. What am I going to do?"

"I'm sure they'll work out a payment schedule."

"You think so?"

"I seriously doubt they'll repossess the baby. Everything will be fine."

"Everything doesn't feel fine. I'm afraid I made a huge mistake. What made me think I could be a single father at my age?"

Uh-oh. "Listen, give me twenty minutes and I'll be there, and we can figure this out together. In the meantime, just breathe. A long breath in, a slow breath out."

I called Levi, who agreed to come by to finish locking up for me, since I was alone at the Zoo that afternoon. Tank was scheduled to come in later for the overnight shift but wasn't available for another three hours. Levi also said he'd drop Charlie and Lambda off at the boathouse so I could go directly to the hospital. I washed up as best I could—after all, I'd been cleaning pens and I was heading to a hospital—then headed out of the door.

"How's she doing?" I asked Jeremy less than twenty minutes later.

"I don't know. They've been in there a long time. Too long." Jeremy looked like hell.

"I'm sure everything's fine. What exactly did the doctor say?"

"He said the baby was too big and Gina was too small for a natural birth. Gina totally freaked when she realized she might end up with a scar."

"I'm sure the doctor will take her career as a swimsuit model into account and be extra careful."

"Gina is going to kill me. And she should." Jeremy got up and began pacing again. "I made her do this."

"You didn't make her. It was her choice."

"Maybe, but I persuaded her to do it. Now she's in surgery and my baby could be in danger, and I have no idea what I'm going to do when I get home with such a tiny person. I'm sure she'll have to be fed, and then there are the diapers to consider. I've never changed a diaper. And what if I do it wrong and she gets a rash? Or colic? I hear babies get colic."

"I thought Ellie was going to stay with you for a few days until you got on your feet."

"She said she would, but with her sandwich shop just opening, I hated to ask. She seems really busy."

Jeremy had a point. Ellie's shop opening the same month Jeremy's baby was born wasn't ideal. Still, I was sure Ellie would help out as much as she could.

"How about Jessica? She's been as excited about the baby as anyone. I'm sure she'd be delighted to help out."

"She did offer."

"Okay, so we'll call her and set something up. Trust me, you're going to be a great dad."

"You think so?"

"I know so."

"I have no idea how I'm going to feed a baby *and* make payments to the hospital."

"How about we worry about one thing at a time? For now, let's make sure Morgan gets born and everyone is okay, and then we can worry about feeding and diapering her, and only then will we worry about the hospital bill."

Jeremy stopped pacing and sat down next to me. He took a deep breath and let it out slowly, as directed. It seemed what I'd learned in the birthing class I was taking with Mom was good for all sorts of things.

"Okay," he said. "We'll take this one step at a time. And thanks."

"That's what friends are for."

"Mr. Fisher?" A nurse I didn't recognize came into the room. "Your daughter is healthy and waiting to meet you."

"And Gina?" Jeremy stood up.

"Sleeping, but she'll be fine. She's asked not to have contact with the baby beyond this point, so we'll need to discuss what's to happen next. Do you have help once you get home?"

Jeremy looked at me.

"He does," I answered. One way or another, I'd make sure of that.

"Then I don't see why Morgan can't go home on Sunday. We'd like to keep her a couple of days to monitor things. She had a tough time of it, but it looks like she'll be fine. You can stay with her for as long as you'd like. The nurse will show you how to feed and diaper her."

Jeremy sighed with relief. "Thank you so much." He turned and looked at me. "Do you want to see her before you go?"

"Of course I want to see her. It's okay?" I asked the nurse.

"I don't see why not. Both of you, please follow me and I'll show you where to wait. A nurse will bring her out to you."

"Wow, she's so beautiful," I whispered as Jeremy sat on the edge of a bed in an empty room and nervously held his new daughter. "All that dark hair and those chubby cheeks."

"She really is something."

"I don't want you to worry about anything," I assured Jeremy. "I'll make some calls and make sure that someone will be there to help you for the first few days. I'm sure Ellie will be happy to stay with you and help when she's not at work, and if for some reason Jessica can't help out during the day, I'll find someone who can."

"Thanks, Zoe. Do you want to hold her?"

Did I? She was so tiny, and I'm such a klutz.

"She won't break," Jeremy assured me.

I held the tiny baby in my arms and gently rocked her back and forth. She was absolutely the most perfect baby I had ever seen. She was warm and soft and smelled so good. I started to imagine rocking my own perfect baby . . . and then she started to cry. I handed her back to Jeremy and resolved to wait on childrearing for a very, very long time.

The moment I entered my mom's new home to pick up Sophie she grabbed me by the arm and pulled me down the hall to one of the spare rooms. "Look what Sophie and I did," Mom said proudly.

Lying on a blanket in the corner of the room was Sophie with four adorable little puppies. "You and Sophie did this all by your selves?" I teased.

"Well, Sophie did most of it," Mom admitted. "But I helped, and when you didn't answer your phone, I didn't panic."

It was odd, but in spite of Mom's worldly experience, in this instance I felt like the parent congratulating the child. Mom had traveled extensively and was well versed in many things, but it was clear by everything I'd discovered in the past few months that her comfort level with childbirth—or, in this case, puppy birth—and childrearing were completely outside her comfort level.

"Good for you," I complimented. "Where was Dad during all of this?"

"In the living room. We decided we didn't need a repeat of the fainting incident."

"Good call. Where is he now?"

"He went to pick up some dinner. Aren't they perfect?" Mom really did seem like a proud grandmother. "When I realized that Sophie was in labor, I moved her in here and made sure she was comfortable. And then, when the first puppy started to come, I sat next to her and reminded her to breathe. I thought I was helping her, but it turns out she was really helping me."

"How so?" I asked.

"I hate to admit it, but the closer it's gotten, the more scared I've been about Harper's birth. I know she's not my first, but you were born so long ago, and I was so hopped up on drugs that I don't remember a lot about it. During the past few weeks, I was really beginning to doubt my ability to do it naturally this time, but then I watched Sophie as she panted and relaxed through the contractions, and suddenly, I knew exactly how childbirth is *supposed* to be. I'm not scared anymore. I really feel that Sophie showed me what to do better than weeks and weeks of classes."

"I'm glad." I hugged Mom. "I guess we should find a box or some way to transport these little guys back to my house."

"Can they stay?" Mom asked.

"Are you sure? You're going to be having your own baby in a couple of days. Are you sure you want to take care of puppies as well?"

"Sophie seems to know what she's doing, and somehow her presence calms me. If it gets to be too much, we can move them later."

"Okay, if that's what you want."

"It really is."

Chapter 12

Saturday, April 19

I got up early on Saturday morning and headed over to Dirk Pendleton's. His housekeeper had indicated that he might be home the previous evening, and I wanted to catch him before he left again. When he answered the door in nothing but boxer shorts, I realized that the children of movie stars most likely slept as late as their parents.

"I'm so sorry to wake you," I gushed. I tried not to stare but found that no matter how hard I tried, I couldn't look away.

"Zoe? Right?"

"Yeah, Zoe is me." *Zoe is me?*

"Can I help you with something?"

I took a deep breath and tried to get a grip. Dirk Pendleton Junior was just a man, not some sort of superhero or god. My complete inability to form coherent words was ridiculous. "I wanted to speak to you about Porter Blakely's murder, but I can see that you're naked. I don't mean naked, I mean almost naked. No, that's not what I mean either."

"How about I go to find some pants and meet you in the living room?" Dirk chuckled.

I didn't have access to a mirror, but I'm sure I was quite red by this point.

"Yes, you're perfect."

Dirk laughed and walked away.

Yes, you're perfect? Zoe, you idiot. I'd meant to say that would be perfect. I never should have come without Zak for backup.

"So you had some questions?" Dirk set a cup of coffee in front of me. I know this is hard to believe, but the man looked even better dressed in faded jeans and a light blue T-shirt than he had when he opened the door.

"Yes," I squeaked. I took a sip of coffee and cleared my throat. "I spoke to Frank Valdez. He filled me in on the cartoon bandits, and it occurred to me that at least two of the costumes used were of movie-wardrobe quality."

"You think I killed the guy?"

"No. At least I hope not. Did you?"

"No. I was nowhere near the bank when the whole thing went down."

"But you did supply the Darth Vader and space ape costumes?"

"I did. A friend asked to borrow them and I agreed to lend them. I can assure you that my participation in the lame attempt to get even with Blakely began and ended with that."

"Will you tell me who you lent the costumes to?" I asked.

Dirk appeared to be considering my question. "Are you sure you want to know? It occurs to me that knowing might be dangerous."

"I want to know," I stated firmly.

"Brave girl. I like that. You single?"

"Not at all."

"Too bad. I lent the costumes to my neighbor, who told me that she needed them for a costume party."

"She? You lent them to Megan?"

"I did."

"And do you know what she did with them? I mean, they had to be much too large for her to wear herself."

"She wanted one for a guy named Carson and the other for some guy named Brady."

"Do you happen to know their last names?"

"I don't."

"Do you know who wore which costume?"

"Again, I don't. I lent her the costumes and that was the end of it. Come to think of it, I never did get them back."

"It's important that I track down the men who wore the costumes. If you think of anything else, will you call me?"

"Sure. Just jot down your number on this napkin."

I did as requested and then left. *Dirk Pendleton has my phone number.* I wanted to swoon but then realized I was being ridiculous. I had Zak; I loved Zak. Perhaps it was time for him to come home and remind me of that.

After I left Dirk's, I headed to the Zoo. Tiffany was going to put in extra hours so I could give Jeremy the next two weeks off, and I wanted to check in with her before heading home. "Hey, Tiff, how's it going?"

"Really good. There's really only one thing I need help with. Someone from the Forest Service called and said that they needed both you and the representative from Fish and Game who responded to the call about the mama bear that was hit and killed to sign the report."

"Darn. I guess in all the confusion getting the cubs settled, I forgot. Anything else?"

"No, everything is going smoothly. Bobby is in the back cleaning the cages, and Tank stayed over to help him. I think Tank is a lonely guy. I told him that I wasn't sure I could approve the extra hours for him to help Bobby, and he said he didn't care about the money, he just wanted to hang out. Apparently, Gunner has a new lady friend and Tank is feeling left out."

"I can see how that would be tough. I'll pop back and say hi to them after I give Colin a call about the report. I hope to take tomorrow off, if you and Bobby can handle the care of the animals. The Zoo will be closed, so all you'll have to do is come in the morning to feed and exercise them and then come back at the end of the day and do the same."

"Bobby and I will handle everything. Have you seen Jeremy's new baby?"

"I have. She's adorable."

"I can't wait to meet her. I thought I'd stop by the hospital after we close for the day. Morgan Rose is such a pretty name."

"Yeah, I really like it. Did the guy from Bryton Lake show up to adopt the sheltie we were holding?"

"Yeah, and he seemed thrilled with her. I think it will be a good match."

I loved the fact that Tiffany was already beginning to refer to adoptions as matches or pairings. It's very important to Jeremy and me that every animal left in our guardianship find the perfect home for his or her size and temperament.

After I finished talking with Tiffany, I headed into my office. I pulled out my address book and scanned for Colin's personal cell phone. Colin Brady was listed under the Cs rather than the Bs. I do tend to list people by their first rather than last name. Colin's name was just under that of the man who Dad and Mom were buying their house from, Carson Worthington. *Carson and Brady.* Dirk had said the costumes were for people named Carson and Brady. Colin had told me he couldn't retire due to finances, and Carson Worthington was on the list we'd gotten of people Blakely had scammed. Last night, when I was at Dad and Mom's for dinner, we'd gone into the basement to look for some old blankets to use to make a more permanent bed for Sophie, and we'd noticed that Carson had left some personal items behind. Dad intended to call him and remind him about them sometime today.

I pulled out my cell. I hoped I was able to get hold of them before my mom and dad invited a killer into their home.

"Dad . . ." I began as soon as my dad's cell was answered.

"I'm afraid your dad is tied up."

"Who is this?" I demanded.

"I think you know who this is."

"You leave my parents alone. They have nothing to do with any of this."

"Your parents are fine, and they will continue to be fine as long as you can get here in the next ten minutes."

"I'm on my way."

"Don't hang up," Carson instructed. "I want you to keep this line open and continue talking the entire time until you arrive at the house. I can't have you calling the sheriff."

"Okay, but don't hurt them."

"I'll be listening, so don't tip anyone off about where you're going or your parents are toast."

"I won't say anything, just don't hurt them."

I told Tiffany that I remembered I was late for an appointment and left immediately. I did as Carson instructed and talked and sang the entire time I was in the truck. I made the ten-minute drive in five and ran into the house.

"Where are they?" I demanded.

"In the basement."

"Are they okay? You didn't hurt them?"

"They're fine. I have no intention of hurting anyone. I simply need to detain you until I can get away." Carson led me to the basement, then tossed in an armful of blankets after me before locking the door from the outside.

"Are you okay?" I ran over to where my dad was sitting on the floor, holding my mom.

"We're okay," Dad assured me, "although your mom is in labor. Has been since he locked us down here."

"I can't believe Carson locked you in knowing Mom was in labor."

"I don't think he knew. At least we didn't tell him," Dad informed me.

I spread out the blankets and Dad made Mom as comfortable as he was able. "It's going to be okay," I assured her.

"I know it will."

I worried about the fact that she was sweating, but she smiled bravely.

I looked at Dad. "You stay with Mom and I'll see what I can find in these boxes to help with the delivery, if need be."

"Delivery?" Dad looked like he was going to pass out.

"On second thought, why don't you help me look thorough the boxes?" I took Dad by the arm and led him across the room. I lowered my voice so Mom couldn't overhear our conversation. I turned, took him by the shoulders, and looked him in the eye. "Mom is in labor. No one knows we're here. Zak won't be home for at least two hours, and even then he may not think to start looking for us right away. We may need to deliver this baby."

"But I can't."

"You can and you will. You have to do it."

Mom let out a moan from her location across the room.

"Okay, you're right." Dad took a deep breath. "I can do this. What do you want me to do?"

"We need to make Mom comfortable and keep her as calm and warm as possible. I want you to keep it light. Talk to her, but don't let her know that you're scared. Tell her the story of the basement we were locked in on Valentine's Day, and how much the blanket she made for you made you think of her. I'm going to go through these boxes while I try to figure out what to do."

"Do you have your phone?" Dad asked.

"No, he took it."

"What if something goes wrong? Your mom really should be in a hospital."

"Hospitals are for amateurs," I said, trying for a light tone. "Women have been having babies for quite a few years now, and I just so happen to be a proud graduate of the birthing academy."

"You mean the class you took? I'd hardly call that an academy."

Mom let out a sharp screech as another contraction took hold.

"Go." I shoved my dad toward her. "And remember, keep it light."

Dad sat on the floor with Mom's head cradled in his lap and told her stories. A few must even have been funny because I actually heard Mom laugh a few times.

The boxes mostly held junk, but there were a few things that might come in handy, including some old clothes and a sewing kit. I prayed that someone would find us before I was faced with the decision of whether or not to use that sewing kit. I tried to act brave for Mom and Dad's sake, but the truth of the matter was, I was scared to death.

"Don't worry," Mom assured me. "It's going to be fine."

"I know it is. What happened?" I asked after I'd done pretty much everything I could for the time being. "Why did he lock you down here?"

"I called Carson about the stuff in the basement," Dad explained. "He said he was heading out of town but would pick the stuff up on his way. When he arrived, he seemed to be in a hurry, so I offered to help him load his truck. While I was loading some boxes of glassware into the extended cab, I noticed something on the floor under the seat. I pulled it out and looked at it. It was a gorilla hand. I remembered what you'd told us about the gang who robbed the bank, and I guess I must have gasped before I had a chance to monitor my reaction. Carson realized I knew what the glove meant and made us come down here. He said he didn't want to have to kill us, but he was on his way out of the country and couldn't have us notifying the authorities until he got away. I guess he figured someone would come for us eventually."

"And someone will," I assured Dad.

"But not in time." Mom gasped. "I think we're close."

I looked at Dad. "Help her get off her slacks and cover her with a blanket. Then I want you to lean against the wall with Mom between your legs. Let her lean against you. I'll see if I can get a feel for where we are in the process."

"Have you done this before?" Mom asked.

"Sure, lots of times."

"With a baby?"

"Not a human baby. I've delivered lots of little animal babies, though. I mean, how different can it be?"

Mom actually smiled. "I'm so proud that I have such a brave daughter."

A brief exam confirmed that Mom was ready to start pushing. I took a deep breath, said a quick prayer, and instructed her to do so. I was proud of Dad, who talked her through the breathing like a pro. Once he focused his attention on Mom, he forgot all about his fear and his aversion to blood.

"Just a little more," I encouraged as Mom leaned against Dad and I supported her legs while she pushed with all her might. "Okay, wait," I said, releasing her legs. "I see the head. I want you to pant, but don't push."

"But I have to push."

"No," I insisted. "You don't."

I made sure the baby was in the proper position and free of obstacles, then instructed Mom to push once more. My brand-new baby sister slid into my hands. She had ten toes and ten fingers, a dusting of light hair, and the lungs of an opera singer.

"Why is she crying?" Dad asked.

"She's just letting us know she's arrived." I wrapped the baby in a blanket and handed her to my mom. Then I let Mom and Dad greet their new baby while I took care of the cleanup."

"She's perfect," Mom whispered.

"She really, really is." Both Mom and Dad were crying.

I was trying to decide what needed to be done next when I heard sirens in the background. I used every ounce of energy I had left to pray that the sirens were headed our way. When I heard footsteps overhead, I began to sob. It had been a long and emotional day.

"How did you know we were in trouble?" I asked Zak when he rushed in with the paramedics.

"Carson grew a conscience and called me. He suspected your mom might be in labor and didn't want anything to happen to the baby."

"You caught him?"

"No. He was in the air before he called."

"He killed Blakely."

"I know; he admitted as much. He said he didn't mean to, but he wasn't used to the gun and it went off. He feels bad, but not bad enough to spend his life in jail. I doubt we'll see him again."

"If he was on his way out of the country, why stop to get his stuff? I mean, he took a pretty big risk, and for what? Some glassware?"

"Actually, what he wanted were the photo albums that were in the other box. I gather they're from several generations of Worthingtons. He realized he wouldn't be able to come back into the country once he left, so he decided it was worth the risk to stop by after your dad called and reminded him that he'd left them here."

"So what happens with the sale of the house?"

"I bought it from Carson before your parents moved in. It was part of a deal we made. I didn't tell your dad because I was afraid he wouldn't go for it, but it's actually me that's financing the house."

"Yeah, it might not be the best idea to tell Dad, although I'm pretty sure that with everything that's happened, it'll come out."

"It looks like the ambulance is leaving," Zak informed me. "Let's follow them. I'll drive."

Chapter 13

Easter Sunday

Easter dawned bright and sunny. At least I *think* it was bright and sunny. Truth be told, Zak and I had enjoyed a late celebration the previous evening and were sleeping in that morning. I might not have opened my eyes as of yet, but I could feel the sun shining in through the bedroom window and hear the Mountain Chickadees serenading the coming of spring.

"Happy Easter." Zak kissed me slowly on the lips.

"Hmm." I kissed him back but still didn't open my eyes, wanting to cherish the moment.

"If you don't get up, you won't be able to see what the Easter dogs brought."

"Easter dogs?" I opened my eyes. Charlie and Lambda had joined us on the bed, and both had bunny ears attached to their heads. I sat up, and Charlie climbed into my lap while Zak handed me a beautiful basket filled with all sorts of yummy delights.

"You got me an Easter basket?" I was pretty sure I was going to cry. It had been years since I'd had an Easter basket, and not only had Zak taken care with each selection, but he'd tied it up with a huge ribbon in my favorite color.

"The basket is from the Easter dogs," Zak corrected me.

"Well, thank you very much." I hugged both dogs, then encouraged them off the bed before turning to show my appreciation to Zak.

"Not yet." Zak kissed me. "Open the eggs. The eggs are from me."

Inside the basket were three plastic eggs. One was yellow, one was red, and one was purple.

"Open the yellow one first," Zak said.

I did as instructed and pulled out tickets to a Broadway show. I looked at Zak with a puzzled frown on my face because we didn't live anywhere near New York City.

"I have to go to New York next month to take care of some business, but this time I thought you could go with me," Zak explained.

"Really?" I smiled.

"Really."

"Will Belinda be joining us?" I hoped Zak's beautiful assistant would be sitting this trip out.

"Belinda no longer works for me," Zak informed me. "I thought I mentioned that she got married and moved to France. Married a man we met on one of our business trips, actually."

"I guess you forgot to mention that." The fact that Belinda was no longer in the picture was the best Easter gift I could have received. I'm not sure why I could never get over my jealousy of the woman Zak insisted was just a business colleague and friend. Perhaps it was the fact that at times she spent a lot more time with him than I did.

"I would love to see New York." I hugged Zak. "I've never been to the East Coast."

"And I'd love to show it to you." Zak grinned. "I can't wait to share my favorite restaurants and my favorite museums. We can take a carriage ride in the Park and dance the night away at a club. I've booked us a suite at one of the best hotels in the city. A very romantic suite," Zak added.

"I can't wait."

"Open the red egg next," Zak said.

"There's more?"

"Just a small token. I hope you like it." Zak looked and sounded nervous.

Inside the egg was a sapphire necklace with a *very* large stone.

"This is too much," I gasped as I lifted the beautiful necklace out of the egg.

Zak looked uncertain. "I know you don't like extravagant gifts, but I saw the necklace and pictured you wearing it. Please let me give this to you. It matches your eyes perfectly, and when I saw it, I knew it was created especially for you."

It was beautiful and I could see that this was important to Zak, and he certainly could afford it, even though I would probably have been just as happy with a much smaller stone. I was pretty sure I was going to cry, so I wrapped my arms around Zak's neck and kissed him in lieu of a thank-you. He lifted my hair and secured the clasp around my neck.

"There's one more." Zak handed me the purple egg.

"Zak, I really can't. You've already given me so much."

"Open it." Zak grinned.

I held my breath and opened it, hoping it wasn't another extravagant gift. "A feather?"

By the time Zak finished showing me exactly what the feather was for, it was well into midmorning. He made breakfast while I showered and dressed for the play and the egg hunt. We planned to stop by the hospital to visit both Harper and Morgan before we headed to the community center. Morgan was supposed to be released later in the day, but Zak and I wanted to visit while we had the chance.

"Another glass of champagne?" Zak asked as I nibbled on the strawberry I found in my first glass.

"I really shouldn't. I'd hate to show up at the play sloshed. These pancakes are really good. Do I taste macadamia nuts?"

"It's my mom's recipe, which includes nuts and dried cranberries."

"They're really good." I looked out at the clear blue water just beyond the sand that separated Zak's deck from the lake. "It's such a beautiful day. I'm kind of sorry we can't just lie on the beach and veg. It's been such an insane week."

"We could stay home," Zak said.

I was tempted to do just that as I watched Charlie and Lambda play in the water.

"We need to go by to check on Sophie and her pups. Dad went home last night after Mom and Harper went to sleep, so I'm sure they're fine, but I promised Mom. She's really bonded with the little dog."

"And you did promise to go by the hospital to visit this morning," Zak reminded me.

"I did, which means," I looked at the clock on the back wall of the house, just outside the sliding door, "that I should finish getting ready since we're already into afternoon."

"You look ready to me," Zak commented.

I held up one leg to reveal a bare foot.

"I guess you should wear shoes. I'll clean this up and start the truck."

When we arrived at the hospital, I went to visit with Jeremy and Morgan, while Zak saw to Jeremy's bill. I wasn't sure how Jeremy was going to take the news that Zak intended to pay it in full, but in the end, I was pretty sure he'd be relieved not to have to begin his life with Morgan deeply in debt.

"You brought Morgan an Easter basket." Jeremy smiled when I walked through the door of the room he'd been using with a giant basket tied with a pink bow and filled to the brim with baby supplies, as well as a stuffed doggie.

"It *is* Easter. How's the little princess doing today?"

"She's perfect," Jeremy gushed as we peeked into the bassinet where Morgan was sleeping. She really was an adorable baby, with chubby cheeks and tons of dark hair. "The nurse said I can take her home once the doctor checks her over. I'm really excited *and* really nervous."

"Jessica and Rosalie are waiting for you at your apartment," I assured Jeremy. "And I spoke to Phyllis, who has assured me that you can move into the town house any time you're ready. Levi and some of the guys from the single parents group are organizing a moving party as we speak."

"You really did take care of everything. How can I thank you?"

"You can run the Zoo while I'm in New York next month."

"You're going to New York?"

"With Zak, who, by the way, is taking care of your hospital bill as we speak."

"I can't let him do that," Jeremy insisted. "I mean, it's a wonderful gesture, but . . ."

"Zak wants to do it. I think it makes him happy to do nice things for the people he cares about. He can, at times, go over the top just a bit," I added, pulling out the sapphire necklace that had been resting against my chest under my dress.

Jeremy whistled. "Wow. Zak bought that for you?"

"I know it's a bit much, but it meant a lot to him to give it to me."

"Then perhaps you should wear it on top of your dress," Jeremy suggested.

"Good point. It's just so . . ."

"Overwhelming?"

"Exactly."

"It's beautiful."

"Yeah, it really is. The longer I look at it, the more I love it."

"I stopped by to visit your baby sister on my way in this morning. She sure is a cutie. It's so awesome that Morgan and Harper will be the same age. I bet they'll be best friends."

I thought about my friendship with Ellie and Levi. "Best friends are the most important thing in the world."

"I never really had a lifelong best friend, like you are with Levi and Ellie," Jeremy shared. "There were different people I considered to be my best friend at specific times in my life, but I look at the three of you and see how you have one another's backs no matter what, and I realize what I've been missing. I hope Morgan and Harper will be close friends."

"I'm sure they will be. We'll start them off young with playdates as soon as they're old enough to play."

"Agreed."

"Everything is taken care of," Zak said as he joined us.

"I don't know how to thank you." Jeremy looked up at Zak as he walked toward us. "Zoe told me what you did, and it's just so . . ." Jeremy looked like he might cry.

"It's nothing." Zak shrugged. "Zoe and I talked about it, and we agreed that it would be nice if she could travel with me some of the time, so we're promoting you to assistant manager of the Zoo and giving you a nice raise and a comprehensive health plan as part of your management package. My taking care of your bill is simply part of that health plan."

Jeremy looked like he might pass out. "Really?"

"Really," I confirmed. "You know I love the Zoo, but Zak has to travel more than I like, and he convinced me that it wouldn't be so bad if I was able to go with him at least part of the time. I assume you want the job?"

"Hell yeah I want the job. And thank you. Both of you. I won't let you down."

"I know you won't."

We talked to Jeremy for a while longer and then went down the hall to give my new baby sister an Easter basket of her very own. Harper was awake, so Mom encouraged me to hold her while we talked.

"She has our eyes," I commented. Both Mom and I have blue eyes with thick, dark lashes.

"And your dad's nose," Mom added.

"She's the most perfect thing I've ever seen." I have to admit I was completely smitten with my sister. I'd never been a human-baby type of person before Harper was born. Ellie loved babies and small children from an early age and babysat her way through junior high and high school, while I was drawn more toward puppies and kittens and other babies of the animal variety.

"We still need a middle name," Dad said. "Harper is made up of a combination of my middle name and your mom's middle name, as you well know because it was your idea. We'd like Harper to share a middle name with her big sister, so that her name as a whole represents all of us."

"You're going to name her Harper Harlow?" I asked.

"If it's okay with you," Dad said.

"It's more than okay. I love it."

"Okay, then, Harper Harlow Donovan it is." Mom looked happier than I'd ever seen her.

"Do you get to go home today?"

Mom nodded. "It seems you did an excellent job of delivering your baby sister. The doctor didn't see any complications from the unorthodox birth."

"I'll come by the house this evening to visit. If you don't think you'll be too tired."

"I'd love for you to come."

"I'll bring dinner for everyone," I offered. "Zak and I are going to the community picnic for a while, but I won't eat much so I can have dinner with my family."

"Did you check on Sophie?" Mom asked.

"I did, and she's fine."

"I told you," Dad commented. I think he was hurt that Mom had asked me to check on her.

"We're going to need to start looking for homes for the puppies," I said.

"Already?" Mom's face fell.

"They won't actually go to their new homes until they're eight weeks old, but we want to find just the right families to adopt them, so it's never too early to start thinking about it."

"It's going to be so hard to let them go." Mom sighed.

"We can't have seven dogs," Dad cautioned.

"I know, it's just that they're so cute, it'll be hard to say good-bye."

"Trust me, by the time they're old enough for new homes, you'll be more than ready to have them move on. Once puppies start to get around, they're a *lot* of work."

"Perhaps, and I'll be busy with Harper."

"Yes, you will, but big sister is willing to babysit anytime."

Harper closed her little fist around my finger and my heart melted. Maybe having a baby wouldn't be as bad as I'd always thought it would be.

The Easter play was heartwarming and funny and probably the best one the town had ever put on, despite the fact that as of the dress rehearsal the day before, half of the little eggs still hadn't known their lines. After the play, Zak and I went to the community picnic and Easter egg hunt, where we met up with Ellie, who was with Rob and Hannah, as well as Levi and his date, Carly Wilder.

"I stopped by the hospital to see the babies this morning," Ellie gushed. "They're so cute. I can't wait to have one of my own."

"They are pretty cute," I agreed. "It looks like Hannah has a new Easter dress."

I looked at Hannah, who was wearing a yellow dress with white ruffles and a full skirt, and skipping along beside her dad as they searched for eggs in the tall grass.

"I saw it and couldn't resist. It came with an adorable hat and white gloves, but Hannah was having nothing to do with the hat and tired of the gloves after about two minutes."

"And did Hannah get a visit from the Easter Bunny?"

"She did." Ellie smiled, "It was so cute to watch her hunt for her eggs this morning."

"You went over early to watch?"

"Actually," Ellie blushed, "I stayed over."

I raised my eyebrows. I knew Ellie was very sensitive about discussing her personal life, but I really wanted to know how it went. "And . . . ?"

"It was nice." She grinned. "Really nice."

"So things are good between you and Rob?"

"Better than good."

Ellie held out her hand, and for the first time I noticed the engagement ring.

"You're engaged?" I know I should have been thrilled for my friend, but after the conversations we'd had in the past few days, all I could pull off was shocked.

Ellie looked uncertain. "Please be happy for me."

"I will." I hugged my friend. "I mean, I am. Congratulations."

"Thanks. I wasn't sure what I wanted, but when Rob popped the question, suddenly everything felt right."

I hugged Ellie again. "I can't believe you're getting married."

"I know. I'm still getting used to the idea myself."

"Have you set a date?"

"Not a specific date, but we talked about this summer. I'd really like to have an outdoor wedding. Something on the beach. Actually, I'm kind of hoping Zak will let us use his house."

"I'm sure he'd be honored to have you get married at his house. Have you told Levi?"

Ellie looked at the ground. "No. Not yet. Do you think he'll be mad?"

"Mad?" That would seem like a strange reaction.

"Maybe mad isn't what I meant. I guess what I should say is upset."

"Perhaps," I answered truthfully. "Things have been . . ." I searched for the right word but came up blank.

"Yeah, I know. I love Levi and couldn't bear it if this made things awkward and strange between us."

"It might be awkward at first, but Levi will adjust to the new circumstances. I'm sure the Levi, Ellie, Zoe triad is as important to him as it is to us."

"Yeah." Ellie smiled weakly. "I hope so."

"You're engaged." I tried for the lightest tone I could muster. "This is huge. We need to celebrate. I already promised my mom I'd have dinner with them tonight, but tomorrow night for sure. You and Rob, Zak and me, and Levi and whomever he chooses to bring, will go out after everyone gets off work."

"I'd like that."

"Zoe, we need you at the judges' area," Gilda said, interrupting.

"I'm on my way." I hugged Ellie again. "We'll talk later."

As I walked toward the judges' area, I tried to be as happy for Ellie as I'd pretended to be, but I was having a really hard time separating my joy for her new circumstances and my concern about the same circumstances. I waved to Zak, who was busy manning the BBQ. I knew how lucky I was that I'd found a man who I enjoyed spending time with *and* who had no problem whatsoever getting my engine running. I hoped that, in the long run, Ellie wouldn't regret the fact that she'd compromised.

As I stood near the bandstand, waiting to decide who had the most eggs from each age group, Levi walked up and wrapped an arm around my waist, kissing me on the cheek in greeting. "Don't you look nice?" He complimented the new dress I'd bought for the occasion.

"Thanks." I smiled.

"I stopped by to meet your new sister and Jeremy's new daughter this morning. Jeremy tells me that you've promoted him and plan to start traveling with Zak. This dress part of your new rich-wife wardrobe?"

"Zak and I aren't married, nor do we plan to be anytime soon. Still, I *am* looking forward to traveling with him, and I guess I'll need a few new things to wear to the types of places he's been known to frequent."

"So you aren't going to turn into a snob?"

"Never." I kissed Levi on the cheek. "I noticed you brought Carly. You two dating?"

"I wouldn't say dating. We enjoy each other's company, but after the fiasco with Barbie, I've pretty much decided to stay away from women who have commitment in their eyes."

"Yeah, I guess Barbie did a real number on you."

"Ellie looks like she's getting serious with Rob," Levi observed as Ellie, Rob, and Hannah all sorted through Hannah's basket.

"Yeah." I looked at Levi. Ellie's news was hers to tell, but I hoped Levi wouldn't say anything insensitive. "I think she is. Are you going to be okay with that?"

Levi stopped to consider my question. "He's a pretty good guy," Levi admitted. "And you were right about Ellie and me wanting different things in life. I've thought about it, and I really just want her to be happy."

"Yeah." I hugged Levi's arm. "Me, too."

"Zak give you that rock?" Levi picked up the stone that was resting against my chest between his finger and thumb.

"It was quite a surprise."

"It's beautiful."

"Thanks, I'm starting to love it."

"Well, I guess I'd better go find Carly."

I watched Levi walk away. Despite what he'd said, I fully expected him to be hurt by the news of Ellie's engagement. I hoped that the addition of Rob into our inner circle wouldn't hurt the relationship we all shared, but for the first time, I realized that, while I was concerned about the prospect of an altered paradigm, I wasn't manic about the idea, as I would have been only a few months earlier. Maybe Zak was rubbing off on me. His presence in my life provided me with a sense of security and balance that I'm not sure I'd ever experienced before. Maybe, thanks to Zak Zimmerman, Zoe Donovan was finally growing up.

Recipes for *Big Bunny Bump-off*

Scalloped Ham and Potato Casserole

Pulled Pork Verde

Chicken Reuben Casserole

Strawberry Jell-O Salad

Strawberry Angel Cake

Boysenberry Bars

Scalloped Ham and Potato Casserole

5–6 large potatoes peeled and thinly sliced
2 cups cooked ham, cubed
1 cup grated cheddar cheese

Sauce:
Melt 1 cube butter (real butter, no substitutions) in saucepan over medium heat.

When melted add:
½ 8 oz. package cream cheese
2 cups heavy whipping cream
Stir until cream cheese is completely dissolved.

Slowly add:
2 cups grated Parmesan cheese (the good stuff)
1 cup grated Romano cheese (add slowly; don't let it clump)
Stir until smooth.

Add:
1 tsp ground nutmeg
½ tsp garlic powder
Add salt and pepper to taste.

Layer ½ potatoes, ham, and sauce in greased deep casserole dish. Repeat. Top with cheddar cheese.

Cook at 400 degrees for 45 minutes or until potatoes are tender

Pulled Pork Verde

Place the following in a slow cooker set on high:
2–3 pound pork roast
2 cans (7 ounces each) diced green chilis
1 tb red pepper flakes
Water to cover

Cook until pork pulls apart easily (about 8 hours).
Shred and use as filling for tacos or burritos.

Chicken Reuben Casserole

In greased casserole dish layer:

6 chicken breast halves, boneless and skinless, dusted with salt and pepper
16 ounces sauerkraut (squeeze excess fluid and cover chicken)
6 pieces Swiss cheese (place a slice on each breast)
1¼ cup Thousand Island dressing (cover chicken)

Bake at 350 degrees for 60 minutes. Serve with mashed potatoes.

Strawberry Jell-O Salad

2 small boxes strawberry Jell-O
16 ounces (about 2 cups) sliced strawberries
1 cup chopped walnuts
16 ounces sour cream

Mix:
1 small box Strawberry Jell-O (made per directions on box)
1 pint (16 ounces) sliced strawberries
1 cup chopped walnuts (add more if you really like nuts)

Pour into bottom of 9 x 13 glass baking dish. Chill until set (about 2 hours).

After first layer is set:
Spread 16-ounce container of sour cream over the top (do not use low fat). Chill for 30 minutes.

Make second small box of strawberry Jell-O according to directions. Carefully pour or ladle the Jell-O on top of sour cream layer; be careful when placing this layer on top or you'll mess up the sour cream. Chill for 2 hours.

Strawberry Angel Cake

Make angel food cake according to directions on box; bake in angel flute cake pan. Cool completely. Cut top off about one-inch down. Scoop out middle, leaving adequate cake on sides.

Mix together:
1 small box strawberry Jell-O, made according to directions and chilled until set
1/3 small (8 oz.) Cool Whip
2/3 pint (16 oz.) fresh strawberries, cut up small

Fill cake with Jell-O mixture; there will be some mixture left in most cases. Replace cake "lid" that was set aside. Frost with remaining Cool Whip. Garnish with remaining whole strawberries.

Boysenberry Bars

Mix together:
2 cups flour
1½ cups long cooking oats
½ cup brown sugar, packed
1 cup butter (room temp)

Reserve 1 cup of mixture. Press into greased 9 x 13 baking pan.

Cream together:
8 oz. cream cheese, softened
14 oz. can sweetened condensed milk
1 tsp vanilla
1 package (8 oz.) white chocolate chips

Spread over flour mixture.

Combine 1 can boysenberry pie filling (or any fruit). Mix with 2 tbs cornstarch. Spread over cream cheese layer.

Sprinkle reserve flour mixture and 1 cup chopped salted cashew or peanuts over the top.

Bake at 375 degrees for 35 to 40 minutes or until golden.

Cool and cut into bars.

Kathi Daley lives with her husband, kids, grandkids, and Bernese mountain dogs in beautiful Lake Tahoe. When she isn't writing, she likes to read (preferably at the beach or by the fire), cook (preferably something with chocolate or cheese), and garden (planting and planning, not weeding). She also enjoys spending time on the water when she's not hiking, biking, or snowshoeing the miles of desolate trails surrounding her home.

Kathi uses the mountain setting in which she lives, along with the animals (wild and domestic) that share her home, as inspiration for her cozy mysteries.

Stay up to date with her newsletter, *The Daley Weekly*. There's a link to sign up on both her Facebook page and her website, or you can access the sign-in sheet at: http://eepurl.com/NRPDf

Visit Kathi:
Facebook at Kathi Daley Books, www.facebook.com/kathidaleybooks
Twitter at Kathi Daley@kathidaley
Webpage www.kathidaley.com
E-mail kathidaley@kathidaley.com

Made in the USA
San Bernardino, CA
06 July 2014